TEN TO
THE STARS

By
RAYMOND Z. GALLUN

I0541490

ARMCHAIR FICTION
PO Box 4369, Medford, Oregon   97501-0168

*For more information about Armchair Books and products, visit our
website at…*

www.armchairfiction.com

Or email us at…

armchairfiction@yahoo.com

TEN SPACESHIPS FOR TEN BRAVE MEN

There were ten of them, brash and cocky for the most part, all equipped with Harmon Pushers, the new individual spaceships that could take you anywhere you wanted to go in the Solar System. So they struck out—some in groups, some individually—toward the unknown. For some it was as simple as going to the Moon. Others felt the alluring, exotic pull of Mars and Venus. Some even felt the mysterious beckoning of the far-off Asteroid Belt. But for all of them it was a chance to meet their destinies in the wilds of outer space.

They promised to meet again in ten years, after they'd explored all of space. It was sentimentality of course, such as kids have always gone in for. Only, out in space, kids turn into men…

FOR A COMPLETE SECOND NOVEL, TURN TO PAGE 77

CAST OF CHARACTERS

GANNET

The allure of space was too much for him, so he threw himself into a life of great adventure. Yet something was still missing…

DEVLIN

Just a dreamer and probably too soft for a space adventure. But was he—in his own way—the strongest of them all?

GLODOSKY

A smart guy, but as accident-prone as they come. Fortunately one of his accidents proved to be a true life-saver.

KATH

She was almost too young to test the wilds of outer space. But she would wait there in the deep void…for the man she loved.

HARWIN

He had been a rugged soldier on Earth. But why would he want to become a scavenger in the Asteroid Belt?

LENZ

There was the desire for adventure within him, but that took back seat to an even bigger desire—to make money.

PHELPS

Flashy, confident, and the only one of the group whose pockets were deep enough to afford a rocket ride into space.

CHAPTER ONE

THE OFFICIAL name of man's pathway to the planets was the Jarmon Jet Engine Number Three, but that lasted only long enough for someone to name it the Pusher. It was appropriate—it pushed men right up from the Earth and out into space in droves. It opened the planets to every young fool who had stars in his eyes and the ability to dig up the small sum needed to put the Pusher into a hunk of tin that could be called a ship. Like the ten who stood in the rain outside the science museum at Hume Hall, waiting to get a sneak preview of the gadget.

There was Lenz, shabby as usual. Beside him was Gannet, always laughing, with the white marks in his hair and the radiation burns he'd got in the recent war. There was Glodosky, the accident-prone medical student, flexing the fingers of a wonderful mechanical hand, which had replaced the one he lost to a freak prewar infection. Beside him, Dopy Devlin, who always got high marks in science, was talking to himself as usual. Tobias was trying to sound as brash as usual, but the look in his eyes said that his motorcycle didn't mean much anymore. Roscoe, the University's star end, simply looked embarrassed, but he was the big, silent type, and that was normal.

Harwin, the ex-soldier, had come up from the rows of olive drab barracks—quiet, experienced, a little swashbuckling. Flashy Phelps had left his sleek fission-driven car parked nearby and money had made him sure of himself, unless you looked too close. Major Benrus, the glamour soldier, might have been a garage mechanic, except for the war. But now the calm force of him couldn't stop pushing him on to victory.

And finally, there was Little Thomas, the last—and maybe the least—of the ten. Precise, silent, truly excellent in mathematics, and about as noticeable as a snowflake in a blizzard.

Like a good-natured impresario, Flashy Phelps now took command. "The caretaker is opening up!" he said. "Let's roll…"

A minute later they stood before the invention that promised to unlock the barriers of the solar system to almost anyone who had the nerve for such adventuring. It was a shiny tube, clamped vertically in a thrust-measuring harness, inside a glass case. Around it, setting it apart by contrast, was the dusty room, dating back to the eighteen-nineties. The other displays had been set up much more recently, of course. But could one ever look at dinosaur bones, apparatus for demonstrating physical facts, of cut-and-dried star-charts, now?

The old caretaker touched a button gingerly, and a tenuous blue flame, a meter and a half long, shot down from the bottom end of the cylinder, causing it to jerk sharply upward in its thrust-harness. The protecting baffle below whitened with heat. The thick heat-and-radiation-resistant glass of the case took on a blue fluorescence. Gauge needles jumped and swung, registering.

"This model Pusher weighs only twenty kilograms," Roscoe, the football man, pointed out. "It says so here on the data poster. But she's showing a sixty-four-kilo thrust!"

"Sure," Tobias affirmed. "And it also says that five hundred grams—hardly more than a pound—of powdered Dynamium, that new synthetic element number 101 of the Periodic Table, is enough fuel to keep it running at full tilt for an hour. It can keep on lifting, and accelerating, more than three times its own weight—straight up. It's like a rocket with no heavy fuel load that burns out in a few minutes!"

"That streamer of hyper-thin vapors, superheated, is so steady that it seems almost rigid," Devlin muttered. "It's hard to believe that it's really moving at seventy percent of the speed of light. It's that velocity that gives the force. Acceleration, going on for hours, could build up to almost any speed…"

Gannet kept staring at the engraved plate on the side of the jet engine. *"Patented November 11th, 1992,"* it said. More than ever he felt as if he were inside some kind of temple to coming history which both trapped and glorified him. The others couldn't feel much different.

"This is just a model," Harwin, the ex-soldier, said hoarsely. "But we've all heard. A full-size Pusher is so simple and easy to make that—with government subsidy because they want other worlds colonized—it costs only a thousand bucks."

To these students, some of them shabby for more reasons than the still-existing shortages, this remained a lot of money. As they were reminded of a price, their faces fell a little.

"Oh, well," Gannet said.

Regret was tempered some by relief. Perhaps the thought was shameful; but if finance kept you from doing a thrilling but fearsome thing, then you were excused with honor.

But restless young minds have always been gifted with a special talent for getting the most for the least.

Devlin's eyes were a bit wild. "Do we have to be stymied that way," he said, "when we know that if we can get the Pushers, we could build our ships with cheap war-surplus supplies?"

Everybody looked at Devlin strangely. He was a book-theorist. A soft, pedantic kid. A high-strung, sheltered screwball.

"Think your money will let you go?" Lenz taunted.

Devlin's cheeks paled. "Shut up, wiseacre," he drawled.

Then Phelps spoke with his usual flourish, saying what he had planned all along, and what was half expected of him by the others:

"I can stake you all to a reasonable amount, without strings, fellas. It's only fair. I can do that much for my buddies."

There was a tense pause, during which each man must have tried to weigh his own courage and dreams against the scare in him. Lenz was the first to answer.

"Thanks, Phelps," he said earnestly. "Count me in."

"Me, too," Tobias seconded brashly.

After that it was like ragged rifle fire.

"I'll finance myself. Pride," Harwin, the veteran, stated.

"Same here," Roscoe, the football man announced.

"I'll be another independent," Gannet declared.

"I can't swing it alone, Phelps. Thanks," little Thomas piped up. His companions stared.

But they stared more when Dopy Devlin growled, "Do you really think I'd stay out of this? Just give me a hand, Phelps!"

He was the defiant Mamma's Boy. The young pedant, the rose petal. How would he survive out there? You heard the stories of what happened even to some stolid people. If he went through with his boast, you felt that it was suicide.

Then there was Glodosky. Not exactly a stumblebum, but with the same effect. The guy whom the paint bucket always fell on, and whom stray baseballs always hit. One of those called accident prone by statistics. A bird with a mysterious affinity for ill luck. What would happen to him under the naked stars of space, away from the mellow scene of a campus?

Ruefully he shrugged a pair of massive shoulders, and grinned.

"You know me, fellas," he said. "But should I stay in bed all my life? Thanks, Phelps."

Phelps and Benrus didn't have to declare themselves in; for it was a foregone conclusion. Now everybody looked to Benrus for guidance. He was the oldest—twenty-five. He knew speed and power. As civilian kids they'd all seen the war. But they envied his deeper knowledge of living. It was a thing that they had to get caught up on.

Benrus' glance was sober and a bit quizzical. The others could hear sleet tapping on the windows.

"Just to be sure," he said. "we'd better each check on what we want from life."

"Philosophers are dopes to wonder what life means," Lenz answered promptly. "Food, love, sex. Getting rich, maybe. And helping to find the materials to make living better everywhere after the war. But sidestep the myth of perfection. The fun of life is in the struggle and the gamble, the seeing what comes out of the years. Being able to look back, feeling that you haven't missed too much—that your memory-mixture is rich, and quite a bit wild. Maybe most of all, life is to make yourself a man…"

"For guys like us, he's absolutely right," Gannet joined in.

He felt the truth of this boiling in his blood. And there were prompt secondings of his statement.

"Ten years from now, to the hour," Tobias said loudly, "let's all meet in this same Hume Hall, and compare notes and adventures!"

This bit of young whimsy echoed, thin and naive, in the big room.

Benrus, the ex-flier, laughed. "Okay—let's," he said.

From that moment, in their minds, they were really on chilly, fabulous Mars with its ruins and deserts, on hot, smothered Venus, or among the crazy, wonderful asteroids, where an inhabited planet had been blown apart, perhaps by a colossal atomic torpedo that bored to its center, to leave the artifacts of its civilization drifting, preserved by the vacuum and the cold through millions of years, in a huge orbit around the sun.

And what went on in the old garage that Phelps rented out of town, was no isolated phenomenon. All over America, and in scattered parts of the recently ripped-up world, the same strange phoenix was hatching, as youth with new technology behind it—some of it war-born—reached for colonization of the solar system.

Here were the ghosts of all the motorcycle, plane-model, and aero clubs of the past, concentrating now on bigger objectives.

LONG BEFORE the ordered Pushers arrived, blueprints from supply houses became the guides for the welding of skeletons of Titanium-alloy tubing, meant originally for the frameworks of supra-atmospheric bombers. In that old garage, ten such skeletons, all about fifty feet in, length, but of varying types, began to take form in a row. Fingers, some of them not as deft as others, blundered, but there was always help at hand. Within these frames, anti-radiation bulkheads, gyroscope rotors, chlorophane air-rejuvenators, and delicate electronic instruments—all meant for the bombers, and now purchased for almost nothing—were fastened into place according to precise directions in the instruction pamphlets.

Then, over the skeletons, went the thick skin of insulated metal-sheathed plastic. Its seams were sealed and rubbed smooth, and tested for leaks. After that, the cabins (usually cylindrical, where a man could only lie prone and strapped to the padding before his observation window) could be arranged somewhat according to personal taste—supply lockers here, water tanks there, pin-up girls here, and so on.

Maybe it was no surprise after all that in the late spring, shy, precise little Thomas completed his ship and bolted his Harmon Pusher into its tail two days ahead of his companions. Moreover, the government safety inspectors said that his craft was the best, and showed the finest workmanship of the lot.

Perhaps Thomas got a bit scared, then. Or maybe hero worship cropped out in him. Anyway he said:

"You test fly it, Benrus. Show us how."

So, on the next Saturday morning, from a nearby vacant field, the war flier took it straight up for a thousand miles, on its thin streamer of fire. And most of the way Benrus' rough laugh came back to the listeners by radio:

"Beautiful ship, Thomas!"

But it came down in a vertical power dive. Benrus' mistake was to fly it manually, instead of switching in the delicate robot controls that spacecraft are meant to use. Perhaps Benrus wasn't as fit as he used to be, blacking out under acceleration at the wrong instant.

Anyway when Phelps drove with the gang for ten wild miles, the farmer told them that his potato field had splashed like water. The hole in the ground still glowed and smoked with the heat of impact. Of Benrus there wasn't much left to bury or cremate.

Just the same, here was Phelps' chance to decide that it was his duty to run the food company he owned, himself, instead of delegating the job to others. Or for Glodosky to remember his jinx and unfinished medical studies. Or for others to consider the worries of their families. Gannet, himself, almost wished he weren't an orphan. Anyway, the key man and main prop of the crowd's project was gone. But for Thomas, it might have withered like a rotten apple.

He had built the death ship. He turned ghastly pale; then green. Then he lost his dinner—which is not a romantic or delicate way to show grief. Two big tears made the mess worse. But he said without phony dramatics:

"I guess Benrus used up all his luck in the war. So I take his ship, *Gremlin's Roost*. And not to Mars, like I wanted. But to Venus, where he meant to go."

What he could do, the others felt compelled to equal.

"Stick to Mars," Tobias urged him later, with a touch of hysteria. "You know that Venus is no lovers' dream. Days and nights weeks long. Crazy seasons because of the extreme tilt of the planet's axis to the plane of its orbit. Smothering heat, then smothering blizzards. An atmosphere mostly of carbon dioxide. No place for anybody but a fanatical scientist. Like living in a dark hole—breathing canned air. Be smart, kid…"

Tobias looked tough and Thomas looked weak. With his nerve Thomas propped the sagging project. And in another way Tobias did the same.

His case headed up several days later, when he brought a dark, fiery, and very pretty little girl to the workshop. Or maybe she insisted on coming.

"I'm here to tell you fellows," she said evenly, "that Toby is through with all this."

Gannet felt the meaning of this scene just as the others must have. An ancient situation. The sweetheart with all of a woman's capacity for gentleness and fury. The guy protected and possessed for his good or his detriment. Because she loved him, and had her own ideas. Because, partly, those ideas were his, too. Kids and a home. Tender, secret moments. Yeah, there was substance to such thinking, too.

Tobias looked sour, shamed, and pleading. Yet he defied his companions and the half of himself that sought to prove his strength and to satisfy a burning romantic curiosity to see the strangest of the strange.

His lips jutted. "I can't help it," he growled. "I'm not twins. I can't cut myself in halves and go two ways. Kitty's right. I'm staying with her. But it's not because I'm yellow! Damn you all—you understand that, don't you?"

"Sure, Tobias," Phelps tried to soothe honestly. "We understand. We'll have wedding presents sent, and we wish you both the best of luck and happiness…"

CHAPTER TWO

BUT THE group's inner contempt had to harden its remaining members. For they had to be above the thing they despised. Gannet wished mightily to escape the stigma of the white feather. And could it be any different with the others?

"Scratch two," Gannet said later. "Benrus and Tobias."

Eight ships hissed up from the rented field the next day. You don't reasonably fly spacecraft manually. Speeds are too great; controlling is too finely timed. Nobody monkeyed with the pilot instruments. So the test flights were all successful. There were no more ruined potato patches to be paid for.

Dopy Devlin came back, pale, but lost in a rapturous daze. "I saw the stars at noon!" he muttered. "And the black sky with the air ripped off and the stars white hot!"

They were all cocky, triumphant, and relieved of brass-flavored scare. Even Glodosky. Though a humble wonder showed in him.

"I got back down, Gannet!" he enthused. "Here I am without a scratch on me! Maybe my jinx is busted. Maybe I'll make it to the Moon with you and Devlin…"

Gannet shook Glodosky's cold mechanical hand, just then realizing that these two would be companions. Phelps and little Thomas were plotting their courses to Venus, as their first venture. Not so good, some thought. Lenz, Roscoe, and Harwin meant to shoot straight out to the Asteroid Belt.

Some minutes later, Harwin took Gannet aside, and gave him the gently insolent, suit-yourself advice of an older man who has faced danger many times, and has drawn shrewdness from experience.

"The Moon, eh, Gannet?" he said with a side grin. "Getting into things by side stages—like some people going into ice water?"

Gannet chuckled. "That's about it," he said. "The Moon's the nearest."

"Um-hmm—that's one way of approaching an unknown that could finish you sometime," Harwin told him. "With caution. Me—I like the long, deep dives better. I already talked Lenz into switching from Venus to the Asteroids. The farthest place, the newest, the best. It ain't the culture of the Old Planet that blew up that's so important. It's that the whole metal insides of a world are laid open for easy mining. You know that the Earth has a heart that is largely gold, too. But who can get at it? And who wants gold, anyway? It'll be almost worthless, now. Think of almost pure uranium instead. The power source of the future is out there. And no end of industrial metals. Come on, be smart, Gannet. I like Glodosky. Too bad a good guy has to be a Jonah. But some of his luck might rub off on you. As for Devlin, when he mumbles to himself I wonder how the doctors can call him emotionally fit."

Gannet felt a sharper twinge of worry. But a stubborn and adventurous perversity hit him.

"I like to do things my way, Harwin," he laughed. "Step by step, not skipping anything. And I haven't seen the Moon. Maybe we'll meet out there in your Asteroid Belt sometime before long."

It was mellow June, and the bunch graduated. Then some went home to visit their folks, and to say so long for a while. Thomas, Devlin, and Glodosky were all under twenty-one, but nobody kept any of these at the last minute, from space. Their intentions were an accepted thing everywhere, nowadays. Gannet was nineteen, but he was an orphan.

Some of the crowd brought relatives back to see the takeoff. Devlin's mother came. And his sister. Devlin's mother was a prim little woman, different from what Gannet had suspected. Hard. But maybe naive, too. She seemed to think her boy was just going on a picnic, when she said to Gannet:

"He's a strange kind of son…"

Kath Devlin was just budding out of the awkward age—with great promise. Her pale brat's eyes dug at the ships with such interest that Gannet said jauntily for her to hear:

"Before we get started, we'd better check for stowaways, fellas!"

Kath met this compliment with a pout and a blush and a look of murder. Too bad for her that she wasn't a boy.

Phelps' smooth Bett was there, and Lenz's Mary. Mary showed the hurt of long neglect. Bett masked her injury with a light and cheerful indifference.

"We used to know each other—for laughs," she said. "Good luck."

Phelps bowed, and patted her cheek. "Thanks, Bett," he said earnestly. But his former sartorial elegance still showed in the neat coverall he was wearing.

The ships started out almost together. With the power of the Harmon Pushers to depend on, waiting for special favorable moments for a takeoff to any given destination was no longer necessary. You plotted your trajectory to fit the time that was convenient.

Two ships flashed sunward. Three arced around the Earth to head in the opposite direction. Three more climbed more cautiously Moonward. None dared to use full power. And all joined the general restless flow outward, to colonize the solar system.

NOT MANY many hours later, Gannet watched his ship slide down backwards on its jets, to a velvet landing by instrument. Then, in a space armor that was really a high-altitude suit for bomber crewmen, he was stumbling about the Moon through the dust of thermal erosion, and through the daze in his mind. The feeble lunar gravity confused his feet.

There was the mountain ring-wall of Copernicus all around him, one half of it shoving the black fangs of undiffused shadows toward the blazing sunlight on the crack-lined lava around his boots. There were the brittle stars and the inky, airless sky. The Earth was high, and fuzzy blue-green, but he had the frightening impression that it was really far beneath him, and that he would never be able to climb down again.

There were the clusters of glinting metal igloos that showed man's presence, even where there was no natural air to breathe. And he was moving toward them. His ears rang with the silence. But in his brain was the thought that he hadn't gone hysterical in space as some guys still did. Even the weightlessness, which felt exactly like falling, had brought him no panic. That much was proven. There was that much growth. He was that much of a man. And to the extent of what was around him, so much of burning curiosity was satisfied. He was on the Moon! This was his personal conquest.

Devlin and Glodosky he had hardly troubled to notice, but now their voices came to him by helmet radio.

"We made it—we got here!" Glodosky was saying thickly. And the words were more pointing out of triumph.

Devlin's tone quavered, either in terror or ecstasy. The sourness in him was gone. "Luna," he was saying, as if in apostrophe. "What was it like when it was brand new—back two billion years? Great meteors falling. Smoking craters. Hot lava. The vapors that might have formed an atmosphere, leaking away into space, because the gravity was too weak to hold them..."

"Yeah—we know," Gannet growled. "Here come the security police."

Martial law compelled you to work, here. That was to be expected, and Gannet and his companions accepted the fact as natural. Even the air you breathed had to be labored for—removed chemically from the oxides in the rocks.

For Gannet it was all wonderful, at first. You slept in a dorm dug deep under the lava, sealed, white-walled, spotless. Your life was as coordinated as the parts of a watch. You ate vegetables grown in vaults, under sunlamps.

Devlin was put to work in those gardens. Glodosky refused a hospital job for ruggeder work digging more tunnels and vaults—extending Earth's hold on its nearest colony. So Gannet and he were doing the same things. Other young men were around them, with histories paralleling their own. And it was good to be building something human and proud.

Gannet kept his high spirits while Glodosky's cheeks hollowed with homesickness, and while Devlin, mumbling, withdrew deeper into himself, causing other men to look at him askance.

Gannet didn't know quite what to do about Devlin, but to Glodosky he said encouragingly:

"Feeling low can happen to almost anybody, pal. You'll straighten out."

"Sure I will," Glodosky affirmed.

But the nostalgia was his undoing. Befogged by it, he wandered right into danger when somebody forgot to put up a safety rail, during blasting. Glodosky's jinx was still around.

Advanced medical science could keep him alive, and patch him up, but it couldn't give him back his own legs. He was fixed up right there in the lunar hospital; and when it was over—well—you couldn't tell the difference.

His legs, now, were like his right hand. They looked like flesh on the outside, even to the dark hairiness. But inside each there was a motor, and many steel cables, and a small atomic battery. Platinum wires finer than spider web were connected to nerve-ends in the stumps of Glodosky's real limbs, to pick up the minute neurotic currents. These were amplified, and used to direct the movements of Glodosky's new underpinnings just as if they were the ones he had originally been born with.

But it took three lunar months. Time for the novelty of being on the Moon to wear thin in Gannet. Time for his mind to get into mischief, thinking of the discipline exercised by officials whose natures were perhaps harshened by the harsh lunar scene. There were the "forbidden" notices. Ah, yes—it was good to dig more sublunarian chambers, but you never got close to anything important.

The great fortress that held all of Earth in range with its guided missiles, was closed to most of the Lunar colonists. Oddly, it was the place that was meant to check future wars, which didn't seem likely to come anymore, but somehow might anyway. Man had grown wary of himself, and of his old hopes of being finally civilized.

You never got close to the great astronomical observatory, either, or to the vast research labs, where more wonderful newness was being figured out, far from the Earth, and where extensive populations would not be wiped out in the case of a major biological accident. Such places were for the elite. Or that was the bitter, inaccurate thought. Thus you never became an aware part of the Moon's greatest meaning in the invasion of space. That was for the experts—those who were investigated and put under contract on Earth. You were of the Lunar bums, the drifters who came on their own, and were always suspect.

Gannet fought such bitter thinking—with scant success. Being off the Earth changed everybody. Or was it life that did that? As soon as you broke its placid surface, and struck out to do something big and dangerous, your view of yourself and everything began to shift. A thing once yearned for could turn to venom inside you. A friend could seem like an enemy. Or vice versa.

In his restlessness he began to hate the Moon. He felt responsible for Glodosky—tied to him. He thought about little Thomas. Deep in Venus he should be—if something hadn't gone wrong. And how about Harwin, Roscoe and Lenz? Out in the Belt! While he was only on the Moon, stuck, left behind, outpaced! He was almost as bad as Tobias and his Kitty and his cowardice.

Glodosky was back, working in the tunnels, for less than an hour when Gannet said to him:

"I'm going, fella—out after Harwin and the others. Maybe you and Devlin better go home."

Glodosky's eyes lighted. "Uh uh," he grunted. "I have my own ship. I go where I please."

A HALF-HOUR after Gannet got into space with the ship that had been stored at the port, two other well-known craft were tailing him. He cursed under his breath. What was he supposed to be, a nursemaid? He could cheerfully have killed Glodosky and Devlin just then.

But being in motion once more, and on some kind of obscure quest, had lightened his inner nature. So after a moment he smirked wryly into his radio and said:

"Okay. I guess you guys didn't "find" yourselves on the Moon anymore than I did."

The acceleration produced by just one Earth-gravity of force, operating for an hour, builds a velocity of something over twenty miles per second. And the Harmon Pushers could do better than that. But maybe it's not so good to go much faster than fifty miles per second, because for one thing, you have to slow down for a landing. Even so, distance is eaten up fast. A million miles in a bit more than five hours.

But Gannet and his friends didn't get to the Asteroid Belt, then. Yeah—the reason was Glodosky. A brace in his ship snapped under the strain of acceleration, tore a big hole in the hull skin, and let his air out. All he could do was lie in his cabin in space armor, and sweat, and sound scared.

No, you couldn't desert him, even if he begged you to—which he didn't. Sixty hours later, with Glodosky almost gone from thirst—since he had had no emergency flask of water inside his space suit—they soughed down through a tenuous Martian atmosphere of nitrogen, mixed with small quantities of carbon dioxide, water vapor, and oxygen. They were down on the wide sweep of the spaceport of a place called Cross Valley soon afterward.

"I'm kind of glad we could come," Devlin said through his helmet radio. "Thanks, Glodosky, for being a clunk—this time."

His eyes were bright and interested in his new surroundings. He kicked at the dry ground, and with a quizzical intensity watched the thin wind (air pressure was only one-point-two pounds per square inch, compared to fourteen-point-five, Earth norm) blow a little cloud of dust toward a lazily turning anemometer atop a gleaming laboratory structure of Earthly design.

Gannet was glad that he was here, too. Cross Valley was one-third several years old, its hemicylindrical corrugated-metal buildings caked with dust; and it was two-thirds yesterday—new and shining. All buildings were hermetically sealed, to confine breathable air, of course. The new part was to meet the needs of the flood of wanderers who had come to Mars by virtue of the Harmon Pusher.

Gannet looked at the town that sprawled in mid-afternoon sunshine from a weak sun not much more than half the diameter—in the greater distance—than it used to have, seen from Earth. Yet its brilliance was undiminished in the frostiness that must be creeping into the air from a high of fifty degrees, Fahrenheit, at noon.

And he looked beyond the town to the umber hills, toward which the trails led in all directions. Young men followed those trails now, to hunt for—well—whatever they found. Wealth, the solution of some mystery, a mood that was yearned for, or death. Nobody yet knew fully what Mars might be good for in the new scheme of things.

CHAPTER THREE

THE FABULOUS Martians had been wiped out long ago. But in return they had smashed even the planet of their enemies. Something ached in Gannet, and it was as cold as the thought of empty pockets far from home—even though he was now flush from recent pay. It was cold and lonely, but there was freedom in it, far from the crowded Earth. The scene fitted the feeling, too. The soft tones of dusty color, and the hard blue of the sky. The peace was that of a small, cold planet, sinking toward death.

Gannet's gaze pulled itself nearer, to explore the vast, flat bottoms of the two valleys that crossed, here—through telescopes they would once have been called "canals," and they may have been artificial.

No water was in them now, of course. There was just a great, rusty mound a mile away—the ruin of some machine. Monoliths loomed, wind and dust scarred, until their bas-reliefs were all but obliterated. There were sparse growths that he had read about. They had scientific and common names.

The low shag-trees had paper-dry whorls, the color of an old hornets' nest, faintly patinaed with moss. The grubbers looked like huge gobs of hard tar, left to flatten irregularly in hot sunshine. But they were covered with little crinkles, like lichen. They were hoarders. They stored not only moisture inside their massy forms, but the oxygen that they produced from carbon dioxide—as all green plants do—as well. They didn't liberate it to the atmosphere but compressed it into hollow spaces in their horny shells. Such economy on Mars was necessary. There was so little oxygen in the air. And during the bitterly cold nights the stored supply served to maintain an animal-like tissue heat in them by slow oxidation.

Gannet thought of this, and of many other things. In the town, through the thin plastic of his helmet, he heard muffled hammering. Absently he decided that a homemade space ship, powered with a Harmon Pusher, was exactly like a covered wagon. This was exaggeration.

"Hey, Devlin!" Gannet croaked. "Can I go into your unpunctured ship cabin and take off my helmet, so I can have a drink of water? Before I shrivel?"

This plaintive request aroused Gannet from his thoughts.

"Come on," he said. "Let's try the town. Beer, maybe. Five bucks a bottle. Unless the Harmon Pusher has already cut the cost of transportation. But what the hell…"

They entered a nearby hut by its airlock. There was a restaurant. And because of an inevitable need in a place like Cross Valley, there was also an inevitable friendly man who grinned and said, "Do you birds want to work?"

No—that doesn't have to be a crooked proposition, even on a frontier. Ninety-nine times out of a hundred it must be okay.

Before sunset, Gannet, Glodosky, and Devlin had signed up. Their ships went into storage again. And in the blackness of the night, with the stars blazing, and with Phobos, the nearer moon—not round, but a small jagged chunk crawling eastward among them, they were aboard a crawler—inside its heated airtight cabin—while its caterpillar treads ground at the valley floor and then at the desert, where the temperature must have dropped to eighty below zero, at least.

They rode all night, cross-country, and thin winds covered their tracks by blowing dust and fine salt from oceans that had died a hundred millions of years ago. They didn't know where they were going, except from what Bart Lasher, the driver who had hired them, had said. "A couple of hundred miles west. Wait and see—you'll like it…"

"Yeah—I like it already," Devlin said. "I used to dream of Mars when I was a kid. And here it is. Deserts, valleys, strange life, ruins. Fifty million years ago its people died. In a big scrap across space. And now civilization is coming. Of people. Not—*beings*. Corruption and cheating are here already. The rest comes later. The dome cities. The harmony. The governments and politics."

Devlin talked on and on. But you never could quite tell whether he was being fervent or sarcastic. Sometimes they all dozed—like hoboes riding a freight long ago. But mostly they didn't.

In the night they passed huge broken dams and rusted pumping stations rimed with frost, squeezed out of the dryness by cold. And strange towers loomed against the stars. And in the dawn there was a white haze of tiny frost crystals, lying low in the valleys.

At 10 a.m., by watches that had been retarded 37 minutes and 23 seconds from the daily Earth norm, they arrived at a small camp of nisson huts at the foot of a bluff that was the mound of a city. The huts, dust plastered, were marvelously camouflaged by nature.

They liked being here at first. They couldn't help it. It was so new to them. The bunks were not as clean as on the Moon. But good enough. And the food came from Earth, in dehydrated forms. Water was flown in from the snows' hard hoarfrost of the south polar cap a thousand miles away. Things were better than they had expected, and that was a surprise that lifted them from the dumps. And you expected guys who had stayed here a long time to look tough, didn't you. Tough and full of grouches? It was natural.

SO THEY went to work, digging into the strata of that bluff. Sometimes you used shovels, sometimes fine knives, and sometimes even brushes as fine as a painter of portraits uses. For care was the nature of the work. It was like archeology with a heavily commercial angle. For what you found were exquisitely colored tiles. Bowls of stone or porcelain. Most were broken, of course. But there were ways to patch them together so that the breaks couldn't be seen. But it was important to find all the pieces that you could. For it was hard to make restorations. And then the price dropped, on Earth, in the art salons where stuff like this brought minor fortunes. It was a new fad...

Throckson, the boss, explained some of this, but he didn't explain all of it. Yet it didn't take many days to get the general drift. Throckson was long and lean, and near fifty. And he could handle himself pretty well. And he matched an old mold. The man who had come to a frontier to win wealth and power by whatever means came to hand. Sometimes he still looked the professor of literature that he claimed to have been. But he had a system now. Also pretty cut and dried, in a way. It had no aspects of violence, except for the young roughnecks he kept around in case somebody got aggressively difficult. Otherwise, you did your work, you got paid and fed. And you could quit if you wanted to. Only, no means of transportation was provided back to Cross Valley, the nearest settlement. Moreover, ostensibly for greater freedom and comfort while working, your regular space suits were taken from you, and you were issued a lightweight coverall with an oxygen helmet, suitable for Mars. It really was more comfortable. But it carried only lightweight oxygen tanks, instead of regular air purifiers. And in the cold of the Martian night it would never be any good.

"They'll give your space suits back, too—if you ask for them," a big youth who looked as though he'd soaked up all the ruggedness of the solar system, told Gannet bitterly. His name was Hellers. "Only there's always something wrong with those suits. A tear you can't fix. Or a missing part... Oh, sure—lots of men have quit and started out, crazy mad. Do you think they ever got to Cross Valley? You guess. There's no life for men in Martian air."

Gannet never cursed or anything. Not audibly. Nor did Glodosky. Both looked scared. And sober. And wise after being dumb. But what good did it do? Think, maybe? Figure out an angle?

As for Devlin—well, any time now. He worked all right. He kept the color in his cheeks. But he'd lost four-fifths of his contact with reality. He looked at things with a kind of half smile—but he seemed to look more beyond them, or through them. The hills around. The gorge or "canal" extending away. And he muttered—not even looking embarrassed any more. You could catch what he said, sometimes.

"Sea roar. Surf on beaches. Here. Once. Like Earthly geology. Similar. Not the same. Coal formed in the same way, though. In swamps. Before intelligence developed. Pulpy things without bones that corresponded to the dinosaurs. Blue sky. Rain. The air was never dense, though. Low gravity. High atmospheric expansion. And never a very warm climate. Then the Martians. Things that stood up on legs without bones, and made the first spears… Can you see them in the darkness? Half visible… Gone… It's figured out a little, isn't it? But there's lots more. Fossils. Pieces of machinery. Pumps can be understood. Engines. But much can't be understood. I wonder what a Martian would think a table fork was for, or a lady's powder puff?"

Poor Devlin—made of softer stuff. And what good would he be when trouble came? Well, he'd die fast, anyhow.

And a couple of times Glodosky said, "I wish I was like Tobias. Home with a woman. He's no fool."

Gannet didn't even agree, audibly. It went without saying, now. Aspects had changed, utterly.

NO PLAN of action was made. Events just blossomed out by themselves in mid afternoon, two weeks after Gannet and his companions had arrived. A tough old man took issue with Throckson. It didn't matter what the argument was about. There were too many possible subjects. Throckson knocked the man down, pulled him erect, and repeated the process. The man's light helmet was torn from him, and he gasped in the thinness. But Throckson, with a smirk on his face kept pounding, even after the man's bloodied lips began to turn blue with the cyanosis of asphyxia.

Maybe it was a cold, dispassionate thing on Throckson's part. Part of a plan of periodic intimidation for everybody. To maintain order later. Of course he started a riot. Someone took a swing at him, too, and he went down. Gannet got the second poke in, and it also had good results. Then the pug-uglies went to work, and everybody had to quiet down, or run. Some did run for a ways. But most of them came back to surrender, because they didn't want to die.

Five didn't come back. They were too full of rage to surrender. To knuckle down. There was Gannet. And Hellers. And another big guy with a soft drawl. And there was Glodosky, who might have gone back, if Gannet had gone with him. There was also Devlin, and maybe his motives were the same as Glodosky's—if his mind had any rational motives left.

They straggled down the valley among the boulders and the corkers and the grubbers—those queer Martian growth. Enraged, Gannet, Hellers, and the other big man forged away from camp for almost an hour without thought of consequences. But the sun was sinking, and that meant ninety below zero. Also, their oxygen tanks were low. There was no food or water. Cross Valley was two hundred miles of this kind of wilderness. A pale haze of frost was gathering high in the air, already...

Gannet growled to his companions. "Throckson got free of law out here. It was easy. Why—in a hundred years, when Mars ought to have many people on it, and cities, there probably will be hundreds of thousands of square miles of desert that nobody has put a foot onto. There can't be any law in such country except nature..."

His wits began to come back out of the blur of blind rage. But enough fury remained to stimulate ingenuity. And there was fear of the lengthening shadows, and of frosty cold creeping through the coverall to add to that. The blue shadows. The quiet scene took on the taint of death. But the question of how to breathe was more pressing. Oxygen, Oxygen…

The grubbers had it. If there was any way to make use of it. Martian plants were like Earth plants. They liberated oxygen from carbon dioxide under the action of sunlight. They made starch molecules by hooking the carbon to water molecules drawn from the dry air, too. Photosynthesis. A function of chlorophyll. But Martian plants couldn't be wasteful. Especially the grubbers. They kept moisture sealed in their hard bulbous forms. And the free oxygen, too. They couldn't let it go. It was too precious. To maintain a faint body warmth by slow combustion at night. That was the way they had learned to survive the nocturnal cold, and the harshened climate.

All right—what good was having read about all that? It was like saying that there is iron in most any kind of soil, when you needed to make yourself a knife…

He kept right on going, away from camp, though. He wouldn't go back. Dying was bad, but not a bad enough alternative. He didn't tell Devlin or Glodosky or the others to go back. He was through with that. They were supposed to be grown men. If they weren't entirely that, was it his responsibility? He felt worn out.

CHAPTER FOUR

But the sun sank out of sight. It gilded the castle-like crags of the gorge walls far ahead for awhile after that. But the stars came out brilliantly, and the speck of the Earth, attended by the lesser speck of the Moon, and it seemed a dream that he had ever been to either place. The cold deepened, and gnawed at his fingers and his lips. And after that—well—desperation took him, and he seemed just to follow his nose, doing all he could.

He found a soft spot of dust underfoot, and began to dig a hole into it, barehanded, and dog-fashion. "Dust insulates against cold," he said to anybody who would listen. If you listened hard enough, you could hear on Mars, even through a thin helmet, without the intervention of radiophones.

Then he tore at the grubbers, and threw the pieces into the deep hole. Hundreds of pounds of the stuff—even by Martian weight standards. Then he packed the whole business over with dust, mounding it high, stamping it down for a kind of seal.

At long last he really burrowed—like a worm going into the ground. He pushed dust backward, plugging his point of entrance behind him. He got down a yard or more to the grubber fragments, and with his gloved fingers, he tore them apart. They half exploded with little pops, from the pressure of the almost pure oxygen sealed up in sponge-like cavities within. Maybe it would work. Maybe it was a new invention, sort of. Maybe his companions would catch on to what he was trying to do, and follow suit. He hardly cared, one way or another.

He got his helmet off, and tried to breathe. There was a thin atmosphere sealed up around him. But it was mostly oxygen. He found out that, for the moment, he could get along. There were little dewdrops of water inside the cavities in the grubbers. He lapped at them. And though he wasn't hungry yet, he chewed some of the fibrous pulp, and sucked it dry. There had to be some slight food value at least, in most any plant. The stuff tasted faintly sweet, and there was an oiliness on his tongue. Maybe there was nothing in it to kill him. So this was an experiment. Maybe it could keep him going.

He tore up more chunks of grubber, to free more oxygen. Then he tried to sleep. It didn't work, then. And in an hour, by the luminous dial of his watch, he had to rip up still more grubber parts. Once he succeeded in sleeping—only to awaken from a nightmare of suffocation. That was near dawn, when the awful cold was beginning to dig down to him. By then he didn't have many unused grubber fragments left. His head ached terribly. Well, maybe he'd figured out a way of sorts to keep alive. But as much or more depended on endurance. Two hundred miles! Well—no. Say a hundred and ninety-three, now. They'd already come part way. But he bet that other guys had thought of his technique before. And had any come through alive? Not that he knew of.

He put his helmet back on, and let the dregs of the contents of his oxygen flask flow into it, and dug up to daylight. He saw then that the others had paralleled his scheme exactly. Digging deep holes, mounding up dust over the pulp of the grubbers. And the others had already emerged. They'd even added a new wrinkle, that Gannet figured would have come to him too.

Stuff your oxygen helmet, except for the absolute minimum needed for your head and vision, with fragments of those same plants. Put the helmet on. Start ripping the fragments apart with your teeth. The key point of course was, that on Mars, with lungs full of concentrated but expanded oxygen, you could go without your helmet, and without breathing, for most of a minute. But you had to work fast.

Gannet worked the trick himself, and then said, "Come on—let's go!" One thing was in their favor. There were plenty of the queer plants they needed growing in the flat canal bottom ahead. If that hadn't been so they would have had to try to carry a supply. Which wouldn't last long.

Well—that time might come. If they had that much good luck.

His mood was waspish. His nerves tore at his mind, and the awful desolation around him tore at his nerves. Mars' charm was gone for him, now. And this valley was what you'd call a fertile region—comparatively! What a place to kick off in! He ached mightily to tear Throckson apart. Maybe the fury of revenge in him was the one force that sustained his efforts to keep alive. Sometime. Some way.

Hellers and the other guy were in worse shape than he was. "Three greenhorns we got on our hands, too—Mic," he growled to his companion. "Like having babies to take care of. Especially Mumblehead, here! He was nuts at the start... He'll go loopy at the next turn. Well—you don't catch me trying to hold him down!"

Gannet growled under his breath, as he saw Hellers' twisted thinking. Baby, huh? He'd given Hollers and Mic the tip about the grubbers that enabled them to still be alive, hadn't he? He fought for self-control to keep from leaping at Hellers. But he hated Devlin too, just as he worried about him. Devlin with the kiddish pink cheeks, the eyes with the cherubic look that had lost all grasp of reality, now. And his mumbles that you couldn't hear the words of in that thin muffling air. But he spoke up loud enough a few times, so that the sounds came through his helmet, and across the small distance to the other men.

"Swell picnic, fellas. Nice to be along..."

Every fifteen minutes or so the grubber pieces in the helmets had to be changed for fresh stock. But the march went on. Lying behind some rocks they found a corpse in a Mars suit. He'd managed to steal an extra oxygen flask, it seemed, from Throckson's camp, on some previous occasion. But both his flasks were empty, now. And all that Glodosky, who went through his clothes with shaking fingers, found on him was a crumpled letter from a little place in Illinois. It was signed, Mom. His name was Fetterly. Burt Fetterly. Yeah—take it along for identification. Maybe…

After that the daze began to close in on Gannet. When the sun got higher, aches began to afflict his body. Something like the bends in that thin air, maybe. But you had to keep going. Thirst was on his tongue from the dryness. And the drops he kept licking from inside the spongy cavities, didn't seem to help as much as they must have. Without them he would have been in a lot worse shape.

Sometimes they had to carry huge bundles of grubbers across desolate stretches. Bundles fastened to their backs with fibers torn from the corkers—those strange treelike growths. In the fifty-degree heat of noon, Gannet felt hot and feverish. But maybe the fever was a good thing. He didn't lose so much moisture from his body, sweating.

They bedded down that evening, as they had the evening before. They were near a vast pavement of rusted iron, to which areas of white glaze still clung. Lord only knew what it was for. The millions of years and the thoughts and purposes of rough-skinned creatures who hadn't been men, and who were long extinct, hid that. And who cared now anyway? Maybe they'd covered twenty-five miles that day.

Two days later, around noon, Hellers blew up. Gannet watched it happen as he might have watched a dream that he didn't believe in. Hellers just ran off toward the low hills of the widened valley. His screams turned swiftly fainter. The other man, Mic, took off after him. And what were you supposed to do about it? Try a rescue? Where did you find the energy for that, or the concentration of mind, even if there was any good or any reality in all that? Gannet half wanted to run, himself. Sure, it was an impulse to try to escape. From aching feet and body, and strain that went on and on and on... Why he didn't, then, was maybe that he kind of lost interest. He just kept plodding, with the mumbled conversation of Glodosky and Devlin droning, without words or meaning in his ears.

Every time he replenished the Martian plant-life in his helmet he did so more clumsily, and with less interest, as if he were going to sleep. Near sundown, all he did was give up—flopping over in a faint.

He woke up with his helmet stuffed again, and with Devlin with all the old sourness out of his nature, talking to him very gently. "Easy, pal. We've gone almost half way. We can make it. We can bed down here for the night."

Devlin's voice was scratchy as with great thirst, but his words were perfectly rational. And Gannet found himself almost hating the thought. Devlin the kid, the Mamma's Boy, the crackpot from the start, the soft-headed dreamer, still on his feet, and still—or again—able to talk straight, when this day two guys of large and ugly proportions and long experience with Mars had gone to their certain deaths, raving nuts... While he himself, who had always looked down on Devlin, had worried about him, was also near to coming all in pieces. He met the truth of it now with a poisonous resentment, which said that all the natural laws of human nature were off beam when it came to places beyond the Earth.

But as Devlin continued speaking, Gannet knew that a conviction of Devlin's advantage had been growing in him all the time.

"Listen, Gannet," Devlin said. "I found out that I've got something most people haven't got. All Hellers and that other mug could see here was the terrible desolation. I've been seeing a lot more. Mars as it was way back—just after the planets were thrown off from the sun. Mars with its first life—perhaps in its small salty oceans of those times. Mars in a stone age. Then, grown old, but at the peak of its civilization. Exploring space, even. Establishing a few colonies. Then, Mars at war with its nameless neighbor. To the complete smashing of one, while the people of the other were wiped out. And maybe Mars of the future, too. See what I mean. Reverie and dreams, under control, can be a good thing, Gannet. Velvet padding between you and the harshness. Sure I mumble. It doesn't mean anything. It's part of the reverie. Try it yourself. Now let's get you bedded down…"

Devlin sounded very earnest.

The next day Gannet did try the reverie. He knew what it was, some, of course. He'd felt the charm, but he wasn't quite like Devlin. He couldn't romanticize Mars, right now. But he thought about girls he used to know. And his dead folks, and the country place they'd had. And a certain island in a lake. It helped. And it might go on helping. If he didn't get in too deep. For that stuff was utterly out of reach, now…

But energy still kept dropping lower and lower, under wear and tear. In another twenty-four hours and thirty-seven minutes, both Gannet and Devlin were just about done. So Glodosky croaked through cracked lips:

"Come on. I'll carry you both…"

"Carry us?" Gannet echoed. "How are you so strong?"

"You know," Glodosky answered. "My legs."

Gannet had all but forgotten. His legs. Not of flesh but of machinery. Atom powered. Never tiring.

And so they were able go on. With Gannet thinking a curious thought. That if Glodosky hadn't lost his real legs, they'd be about dead by now. Misfortune adding up to— maybe—good fortune. Life. Cockeyed. Unpredictable. Who could blame anybody for anything?

Sometimes Gannet and Devlin still staggered along on their own feet. More often they were lashed to Glodosky's back by means of a rude sling of vegetable fibres. They still had to stop to collect pieces of the grubbers for oxygen and moisture and a little food value at frequent intervals. And for more nights they had to burrow into the ground to escape the cold. Their consciousness seemed to fade away from them. But here necessary actions became a kind of automatism.

And so, late one morning, the people on the streets of Cross Valley were treated to a strange spectacle. A pair of strong legs bearing three nearly dead men, their clothing grimed with the red, salty dust of Mars. It was not easy to guess that only months before they had been students in a quiet university town on Earth. But some who saw them did guess. For many had had a similar background. They too had joined the vast outward surging and had become part of the colonial impulse that the Harmon Fission Jet Engine had made possible. They rushed forward, eager to help as much for curiosity as for kindness. The weight of three men on Mars was about equal to one on Earth.

CHAPTER FIVE

Gannet awoke at last to the dim hammering and clang of building. He was in a hospital. It was natural, wasn't it, that in this harshness the nurses would be male? Sunlight was on the windows, heavily glazed to resist internal air pressure of an Earthly level. A studious looking middle-aged man came after awhile, and after profuse good wishes and congratulations for Gannet's still being alive, announced his name...Dan Simpson.

"Survival on Mars, Mr. Gannet," he said. "Under native conditions, I mean. You and your friends have found a way. From what was in your helmets, I can guess part of your method. It will be useful knowledge for all colonists, here. A safeguard in case of emergencies. Something that should be standard, published advice, for everyone here, or on the way here. I am prepared to pay fifteen thousand dollars to you three men. And the others said, come to you. There will be royalties as well, of course. So, would you explain your method fully to me, and allow my firm to prepare pamphlets?"

Somehow the thought of commercial things, so soon after he and his pals had escaped from death, irritated Gannet. So did this man's gentle, rather insipid face—Gannet had already forgotten his name, and did not try to remember it. And with some brash carelessness, as of a haughty person tossing a coin to a beggar, he said:

"Sure, friend. Listen carefully…"

But he found a satisfaction, too. At having done a little. Adding something to knowledge. Doing something that counted. It was one thing that people aimed at, wasn't it? He talked on with better consideration, now.

Yet his mind was on Throckson and revenge. He'd go back out there now—with whatever forces he'd collect. Police, or whatever else there was. Break the empire of a frontier baron.

But later, after they'd let him up and out, he found it wasn't that simple. Throckson had taken care of things like that it seemed. The sheriff wasn't interested in anything but positive proof, and they had nothing to show him. Mr. Throckson was a highly respected man here, and they couldn't just take anyone's word against him. Besides, the police were needed here. They were short-handed, and…

Gannet left him, feeling contempt and something strangely like relief. He couldn't understand it, but somehow the trip to take revenge on Throckson didn't seem as important now as it had before. He told the others and they nodded. They stood there in the Mars suits from Throckson's camp, but they were all busy with thoughts that had nothing to do with getting even. Finally Glodosky shrugged, and turned to Devlin.

Devlin mused aloud, "So? I wouldn't mind staying on Mars for awhile. What's it got? Well—not much in available resources. It's half-dead. And cold. But it has color. Romance. That's an easy thing to sell. And the Earth feels so small. And it's getting so that people can make any place comfortable. They like the challenge of doing that. I could stay—help see what we can do about Throckson. Work, too. And maybe try some Martian historical research. But the Asteroids are better. And plenty of folks have more right to get Throckson than I have. He's a damn fool who'll wind up—very soon—smashed and dead. So why should I lose more time and risk my neck further trying to do something that plenty of others are itching to do, anyway?"

"We've been talking about Throckson, Gannet," Glodosky added. "To a lot of people...while you were still out cold. So more than that bird we just talked to knows about what's going on out there. Come on. Down there's the post office. Maybe mail was forwarded from the Moon. From the gang. Especially from Roscoe, Harwin, and Lenz, out there where we ought to be going."

Gannet felt a difference in his friends, now. Something everybody fought to get. Growth.

Devlin, especially, seemed now to have his feet on solid stuff. Out of danger and strangeness, he'd won pride and confidence. He seemed to have found out what he wanted.

Both Devlin and Glodosky collected bunches of letters. But Gannet, the orphan, got nothing at all. In spite of himself, he felt lonely and left out of things.

Both of his companions thumbed through their sheaves of envelopes. Devlin glanced at Gannet. "Nothing from the crowd, here," he said. "Just family stuff. My mother. My sister."

"Same with me. Only my dad," Glodosky stated.

What they shared with him was the disappointment at no news from their friends. The family part they tried to depreciate. And that, he sensed, was out of consideration for him. In his new confidence, Devlin had lost his defensive sourness, too. That was another thing that space had done for him.

"We'll head for the asteroids anyway," Glodosky said. "We know that Roscoe and Lenz and Harwin headed for the asteroid, Ceres."

Gannet shrugged. He had wanted to go out there. He still did. It is what he would do. Still, there was a dull regret at leaving revenge behind.

"Okay," he said. "So now we see if we can buy regular space suits."

They found a shop. Gannet and Glodosky took new armor, still crated after shipment from Earth. High altitude suits they were, really like the ones they had used before. War surplus—but even at the low prices for such surplus, those two pieces of armor used up the better part of ten thousand dollars.

Devlin did a little better. The smaller armor he bought was second hand, third hand, fourth hand—who could tell? Each dent and scratch on it might have had a history. He put it on right away. Then a puzzled smile came to his lips, and extended up to his eyes. His nose twitched.

"Who hocked this thing, Mister?" he asked. "I mean who owned it before?"

The graying shopkeeper grinned. "Somebody that needed a ticket, on a regular space liner," he said. "Back to Earth, or else farther out. I don't recall which. But a talkative person."

"I see," Devlin answered with some awe. "I could stand a larger size, but I'll take this one."

When the transaction was completed, but while they were still all inside the pressurized shop, Devlin beckoned his companions close. The faceplate of his helmet was open. "Make like dogs, you guys!" he chuckled.

They sniffed dutifully. Gannet caught just a trace of a delicate aroma emanating from the armor's interior, and it didn't come from the unwashed Devlin. It was a whispered hint, plying on them through memories of soft lights and music, far, far away.

Perfume!

And on the outside of the suit, over the heart, a red rose was carefully painted.

GANNET AND Glodosky donned their own new armor as fast as they could. Out in the street again, they all tried out their helmet radiophones. But that wasn't their interesting motive just then.

"It could be the effeminate type," Gannet teased Devlin. "Male."

"Could be. Sure," Devlin agreed mildly.

"Or else some blowsy adventuress who'd cut your throat for a buck," Glodosky hinted.

"Or a sweet and tender violet—who knows?" Devlin himself chuckled.

"Not too likely—off the Earth, or even on it," Gannet stated.

"Hey—what are you lugs tryin' to do—discourage me?" Devlin protested mournfully.

"Of course not—we're your friends, and we just want you to be very realistic so you will never be disappointed," Glodosky said. "Of course, probably, the former owner of your suit hocked it for the purpose of getting home to Earth, rather than to go farther. That's a more regular procedure for folks who go broke."

"It is," Devlin agreed airily. "But who was it who once said, 'You never can tell…' So what are we doing, anyway? Chasing skirts as our primary motive? We should have stayed home"

"We didn't have the sense to do that, and now it's too late," Gannet laughed, meaning of course that if they had known about the events that they had just been through, in advance, they would never have had the nerve to start out at all. Now he was glad that they hadn't known…

"We've got to collect our ships, from storage, and I've got to patch up the hole in mine. Then we can get some more fuel and start out," Devlin said.

They did all of that, clearing Mars at midnight for Ceres. Leaving with other Pusher vagabonds and their homemade craft, for the same destination. Most of the other travelers were young, but a few were old.

The stars were very bright and hard and unfeminine. But somehow they looked a little different now to Gannet. There were women around in space, too. Adding another mystery to mystery. Being alive—that was a supreme success in itself—made him feel good. And lightly, for the sake of old-time joshing, which was back for now, he laughed over the radio, and said:

"Just because you got her tin overalls doesn't make her your girl, Devlin." Then, strapped prone in his cabin, against the weightlessness, he slept. The slightly curved course outward was well plotted. The millions of miles reeled by.

Later, much later, he saw the speck of Ceres growing before him. There was a fuzzy haze of light around it— boulders, meteors, dust, wreckage, following lunar paths and encircling it continuously, chained by its slight gravity. There was a glow from its great smelters—metal being the great new industry of the asteroids. But these countless thousands of bodies, most of them too small to be seen from Earth even in the lens of a telescope, ranging singly and in clusters in an orbit almost half a billion miles across, could not be thought of as a single place, like Mars. Distances were too vast. To say that you went to the Asteroid Belt was not a very definite explanation.

Gannet watched eagerly, wondering how much more eagerly Devlin must be watching. This region was legendary. Here a thing that people had worried as a possibility for Earth, too, had actually happened. An unnamed, inhabited planet had been blown to pieces, the latter following now many scattered orbits, around the sun. And Gannet's reveries about the region must have been then of the same quality. as Devlin's. How quickly it must have happened. How cities, and whole sections of country must have been hurled skyward, the flames from the atomic explosion, and from the hot guts of the planet, being chilled. and quenched quickly in the cold of space, so that destruction of that ancient culture had not been sudden and complete. In fact many of its artifacts had been perfectly preserved in the cold vacuum of space, and had made the millions of years that had passed since, mean nothing to them. The handiwork of Mars. Some gigantic torpedo, perhaps. But Mars' people had died too, in that great conflict. Perhaps both sides had fought for empire.

CHAPTER SIX

Gannet and the others had to cut their speed to a crawl as they approached Ceres, to avoid collision with the yet uncleared lesser wreckage of the ancient planet. But they got through to what someone had called BoomTown, safely. At the spaceport the rotating beacon lights were reflected from a square mile plain of almost flawless and polished nickel steel—not imported, and not smelted in furnaces here, either. It had been smoothed as a native granite outcropping might be smoothed and cut on Earth. Nickel steel, the stuff of many meteors, unrusted in the absence of oxygen. And Ceres was like a gigantic meteor—a fragment that had come from deep inside the bulk of the original planet.

After their landing, Gannet, Devlin, and Glodosky, stood in a group by the administration building of the port. Devlin didn't mutter, now. He spoke aloud.

"The theory of planets' inner structure," he said, "materials settling out in layers, according to density, down to the center. Light rocks on top, heavier ones below, then lots of this nickel steel. And at the center the really heavy stuff; in quantities undreamed of on the surface. Gold, lead, osmium. And a whole string of radioactive elements. But on Earth, and on other regular planets, all that stuff is buried, too deep—maybe forever out of reach. Not here, though..."

"Sure—we heard about all that before, Devlin," Glodosky laughed. "Look at the town. BoomTown. A corny name. But honest."

It certainly was honest. It had the air of having been built overnight—but according to a precise plan. And it was still being built, swiftly—and for a swift, efficient life. Scores of huge airdromes, of thin clear plastic, flexible, but sustained by the atmosphere inside, looked toward the airless stars. And there were hundreds of long, low buildings. Factories, hospitals, laboratories, barracks. From the mines of Ceres, on what had been its deeper side in the original planet, came the radioactive metals that powered the post-war reconstruction on Earth and the advance of its industries, followed by the colonial surge into space. From the uranium of Ceres could be made more of the dynamium that was fuel for the Harmon Pushers.

"Even the Moon was nothing like this place," Glodosky remarked.

"Let's not just stand gawping," Gannet advised.

Their ships were wheeled into hangars, and they rode into town on a moving belt with their packs, and they found their way to a name registry office where they were required to put down their own names, and could search for others. The calendar was different here, and arbitrary. There were numbered months of approximate Terrestrial length, divided into thirty watches, measured by the twenty-six-hour Cerean day.

Thus they found the names, and the time of arrival of their three friends. "Fifth hour, third watch, twenty-second month." Long ago, of course, that turned out to be. But the address of the hostelry was also given. "Merret House, Fourth Lane, Second Cross."

IN THE ridiculously low gravity, they almost floated to their destination. Harwin was in the lobby. The ex-infantryman. He searched their faces, which must have changed some. His own features had thinned down some, but his pale eyes still had that light challenge. He wasn't surprised to see them. Just pleased.

"Good thing I came back from prospecting," he said. "Figured you'd be around soon. But Lenz and Roscoe have gone out again. Lenz thinks he wants to set up some kind of business. He's got that kind of a head. Roscoe's just a big lug…"

"Funny we could find even you in a place as big as the Asteroid Belt," Gannet offered, grinning. "I mean it strikes me funny. Of course it's easy enough, as long as you are on Ceres… Why didn't you write to us?"

"Why didn't you write to me?" Harwin laughed back at him. "Don't worry. Same old story of separated pals, wandering. Too much happening. Too much that's new. New people, new things. No spare time. And the past getting a little dim."

"Tell him what happened to us, Glodosky," Devlin said.

"Glad to," Glodosky began.

But Harwin's interest turned out to be only mild. When Glodosky was finished talking, it was his turn to talk.

"What I'll tell you will be mostly a build-up for the Asteroid Belt," he said. "You can find anything around here from a quick finish to fame and fortune—maybe in a way that you could never imagine beforehand. "You've heard this before from the explorers books. Gold? Hell—don't worry about gold! Think of wreckage floating in space—never changed through all the ages, since the Great Blowup. As if a freighter, loaded with household supplies, and everything that makes for civilization, came apart in space. Only it's not our civilization. It was one that was bigger than ours in some ways. Do you know that, on a little piece of the surface of the old original planet, I once slept in what was left of the house of an ancient inhabitant? That house was stout enough not to fall completely to pieces by that shock. And I made what I suppose you'd call the stove in the place work. Self-contained power unit. But I didn't even bring it back with me. The old owner was there, too—dried up and on his pallet, black—with bones sticking out of him, and not human at all. Kind of a leathery sack, with dried out tendrils, and eyestalks sticking out of him. But these are just hints, of course. There are a lot of things and devices that you can find, that you'd have a tough time figuring out. Just floating in the emptiness. Maybe they're whole devices, or just fragments of the whole, torn apart in the blowup. There are ideas in that stuff. Here, Devlin. You ought to be good at this sort of thing. Catch!"

The thing that lashed through the air to Devlin's palms was a maze of wheels and grids and sliding parts in a round crystal case. Devlin looked at it in awe that was like love. Of course he might never know what it was."

And Harwin's voice ground on. "Things you find could blow up in your face. That has happened. Or it could be worth something. Of course there are the metal deposits, too—the mainstay of economics out here. You might as well say it's all like Aladdin's cave. But like that, it has a curse on it. You think you're a good guy. But wander around here for a while and you'll run into a situation where you know you're a wolf and a murderer. That is when death is on your tail, and morals don't mean anything…"

You could see Devlin's eyes light up. This was for him. Even if Harwin was just exaggerating some—as probably he was.

They jabbered on through most of the night. But in the morning Glodosky, the med student, headed for the general hospital. "I'll play it safe," he said as he left. "I've been riding my luck heavy lately. And you know what its like. So I'll play it slow, now…"

Gannet found that Devlin had already left the hotel. He shrugged and went to see Harwin's prospector's gear, put up in a warehouse. When they both returned to the hotel, Devlin was there in the lobby again. He looked fuddled. But he was all smiles.

"Here she is, guys," he said. "Miss Jeanne Pauls."

"Pardon? Who?" Gannet demanded, puzzled.

"Miss Jeanne Pauls. Entertainer," Devlin said with a pained frown. "You know—former owner, and owner again, of what used to be my space suit. I gave it back to her. Jeanne, here are Gannet and Harwin—fellow voyagers, and former classmates of mine."

They greeted her formally while they looked her over. She was wearing the suit, all but the helmet. There was the painted rose. She was cute and blonde and fuzzy—cute as anything you could name. Cuddly, too. But hardly smaller

45

than Devlin. And what was the thought of her now? The roving, reckless eye. The flow of young feminine shrewdness. Maybe she wasn't as old even as Devlin. Chronologically, that is. But Devlin was still a baby beside her.

Now she giggled. "Hello, boys!" she said. "Devlin, you call him. But he's Arnold to me, already. Arnie told me that you thought I'd be headed back for Earth from Mars. Now why would I be doing that if I came so far? And Arnie found me. He checked back all of the women's names for months in the Registry. There weren't so many. And there were only a few hotels listed where they went. I'm at the Woman's YMCA. Arnie came there, wearing this armor. Of course I saw the rose…"

She stopped, and a petulant look of anger and hurt came into her heart shaped face. Gannet knew that it was Harwin's and his own expressions that did it. Of, humor, judgment, and worry for their buddy. And vexation. Gannet thought for a second that this Jeanne Pauls, this pretty little devil, was going to launch into a tirade against him. So he nudged Harwin, chuckled genially, and said, "That sounds like an interesting start, Jeannie. Romance among the asteroids…"

Later, though, he cornered Devlin. "Where did you get the money to buy yourself another space suit?" he demanded, "to replace the one you needed, and gave away?"

"Sold my ship," Devlin answered airily.

"Um-hmm," Gannet commented. "All in a couple of hours time. Boy—you work fast! Or somebody does! Crazy, ain't it—dim wit? A guy wins a little of being man-size from space. And along comes a certain kind of sharp female operator and cuts him to zero. Haven't you got sense enough to see through this Jeanne?"

For a second a terrible fight loomed. But Devlin held himself in, maybe because Gannet could surely lick him.

"Sure I see through Jeanne," he said at last. "I don't say I thought she was an angel—not the regular kind, anyhow. I also see that you're trying to he a pal and put me straight. Thanks. But maybe I see more of Jeanne than you do. She was on Mars. Now she's among the asteroids. Alone. That means one thing to me. She's got guts. Courage. More in a minute than a lot of your 'good' stay-at-home girls have in a year."

There was a pause. Gannet wasn't really taken aback. Because he knew. He chuckled. "You're right," he said. "But does that make you any less a sucker? Don't you want to go along with Harwin and me? I thought you did."

"I'd like to," Devlin answered guardedly. "But not now. Sorry. I've got things figured out. The way I want them to be. The kind of mood that fits me and the asteroids. Maybe you'll see what I mean, sometime."

Just then Harwin came into the room. "Oh," he laughed. "Rare jewels that women are out here, you want to hang onto one, eh, Sonny? Better learn judo, bud. Better hire a dozen bodyguards. Better go for your blaster, whenever you hear a wolf's whistle…"

CHAPTER SEVEN

After a good sleep, Gannet and Harwin said so long to Glodosky, who had gotten the hospital job he wanted, and to the worried and rather puzzled Devlin. It was the parting of the ways, for a while.

Then they were off Ceres, plunging deeper into the Belt. Gannet was a little like Devlin in his quest for the charm of newness. Here was vigor and manhood. And what was better than to be part of the leading edge of progress and colonization, than to be a searcher for resources?

During his first hours, now, he realized the vast distance in the Belt. Deserts of nothing. Not all tiny worlds at fairly close quarters. But at long intervals. And sometimes in clusters. The glamour wore off quickly; yet for him and Harwin some of it always remained; or a different kind was built somewhere inside them.

There were already fifty thousand men in the Asteroid Belt. But how often did you see even one besides yourselves? Nor was the ancient wreckage of the culture of another people as thick in space as Gannet had pictured it.

And you lived in a space suit. Lots of guys didn't even use ships out here. A small Harmon Pusher attached to your shoulder-plate was enough to hurl you millions of miles. For where was there an asteroid large enough and with a gravity strong enough even to pose the obstacle of velocity of escape? You could jump off of the smaller ones, and never fall back, by virtue of your own leg power. There was this much of the mood of fairyland, traveled by means of seven-league boots. But the dark shallows were real. The shrunken white-hot sun was real. So was the rancid smell of your own sweat inside your armor.

Food concentrates were all around you, inside. And you pulled an arm out of an armor sleeve and fed yourself—if you didn't have the cabin of a ship to relax in. But it was a lot the same both ways. You worked so much outside your ship. Water you drank through a tube, attached to a belt tank. Your armor became like your house.

You investigated all wreckage, and all meteors around you. Relative to yourself there was no terrific speed to either. For, in general, in the Belt, you became part of your surroundings. You moved in the same direction, and at the same velocity.

Certain heavy metallic meteors were what you wanted. Some were black. Some dull gray. Visually you could be confused. But a Geiger Counter fairly shouted at you if you were right—naming fragments from near the center of that broken planet. Anything less than sixty-percent pure, you ignored.

Gold was no more worth the transportation than iron. And sometimes it was almost as plentiful. Earth had a heart of gold, too.

Gannet and Harwin loaded up the freight nets, which then trailed behind their ships. A full load on Earth would have been around fifty tons. Out here it was like a great bubble with a considerable inertial drag.

And there were the souvenirs to pick up, or discard. Rails of steel. Or of some kind of titanium alloy. Maybe they were girders. They'd been snapped off by some terrific force. Once they found what might have been the tip of a tower. Inside they found a small square of woven glass-wool tapestry. Its bizarre design in red, blue, and white, would have turned a bum like Throckson green with avarice. And there were little hooks of silver. And there was something that might have been a microscope. And a flat object with one string. It was of vegetable substance, probably. Call it wood. Maybe the whole thing was some kind of musical instrument.

There was a lot more in that curious round tower-top or chamber, which must have been hurled into space like a projectile when the planet it had graced exploded. It was all mashed together against the floor: metal, wood blackened and dehydrated by the complete dryness of space, and crystal. There were substances and shapes that couldn't be named.

Harwin and Gannet took what they thought might be worth something, as they always did. Gannet felt there were ghosts around him. But he felt the thrill of discovery. This was living. This was a high point. And he thrilled to it.

Of course he always knew that if the steady murmur of his air purifiers stopped, he might mingle with this wreckage too.

And that was just one thing that could happen. But it was good to know that you were equal to your surroundings. Yes—good.

Their first load went, not back to Ceres, but on to another group of much smaller asteroids. For from Lenz and Roscoe a radio message called them: "Unload at Refuge… Unload at Refuge… Get fair prices at Refuge. Stock up at Refuge. Refuge, the way station. Follow the radio beacon in…"

"It's the business," Harwin laughed. "That was Roscoe's voice. From football to space, and then back to advertising. Seems as though those birds are even trying to start a town of their own…"

So they saw Lenz again, and Roscoe, browned and casual, but a little scared underneath. Gannet's and Harwin's loaded nets bounced lightly down beside the half-dozen nisson warehouses they had managed to build, and one worried some if this embryo outfit would ever be able to pay at all. But they'd run in supplies. And of course Lenz said, or maybe bragged, sounding like his old self:

"We made out well enough doing what you guys are still doing, to start something better. Now we've got two supply ships started—flying directly to Earth and back. Pretty soon we'll be bringing in prefabricated houses, and wallpaper for living rooms. You'll see… Join up when you want to…"

"Not before, not now, not ever, not me," Harwin pronounced. "Maybe you can interest Gannet. But I don't think so."

The next time they went out, Gannet and Harwin almost had bad luck. Four men just in space suits fitted with Pushers tried to be friendly. But Harwin was smart, and wouldn't bite. And Gannet used a rifle that fired explosive bullets to keep them off. Stealing ships and net loads was a common thing.

And when they got back to Refuge, Roscoe said. "Yeah, I know. I killed a bloke with a blaster. Had to. You know what he was on Earth? Yeah—a grocer. His credentials were in his pocket. And a family picture. Nice wife and kids. And he was okay himself, in the picture. Funny things the Belt does to people. Living the way they do. Not out of armor for weeks at a time. No luxury. Being scared of smothering something. So the weasel drops out. Watch yourselves, you guys..."

Time went on. There were more and more men in the Belt. You almost expected to meet a few, now and then. Refuge showed signs of growing. Lenz, the poor boy, was building his town. And all the business in it belonged to him and Roscoe. But of course this was a common phenomenon, everywhere.

"They're forcing us farther into the wilderness, Gannet," Harwin began to kid.

Not always were they lucky. Once Gannet was far afield in just an armor. And his Pusher went wrong and almost quit. His radio was too weak for an SOS back a million miles. Lucky his air purifier cartridge was okay. Food and water was the problem. So what did he do. Well, you know what they say in the belt. "You can find anything." He knew what to look for. He'd seen them before. Flat containers of thin sheet metal. There's a little airlock under the arm of each space suit, for the entrance or exit of any object. The pasty stuff in some of those containers made him sick, and the sour liquid in others made him dizzy. But taking his time, he limped back to Refuge all right, and laughed with his friends.

He had a funny feeling, though. Something which kept telling him—only just so long. Sooner or later...

Lots of things happened. Harwin and he might have stolen supplies themselves one time when they were far afield and low on food. Some men had passed though the space lane near them, and glared at them, making some uncomplimentary comments via helmet radio. Harwin and Gannet didn't move against them, but the old cutthroat impulse was there…

They'd been out from BoomTown on Ceres a year then. And then Glodosky finally wrote:

Dear Gannet:

I haven't heard from you. Maybe you're in or around Refuge, which we hear about. Lenz's project, eh? Could be. I'll just take a chance. I'm sending him and old Harwin letters, too. Hope this finds you, and finds you prosperous enough to snoot an old friend. But I know how you are about letters, Pal. So I'm kidding.

I'm in the same place—same hospital. And in spare time in research branch. Electro-neuronics—artificial body parts section. You know how I got into that, don't you? My legs and my hand. All news is good, so far. And there's more good news. But first there's some bad.

I had a letter from Little Thomas. He's doing research work for an outfit on Mercury, now. What he tells me is that old Flash Phelps was killed on Mercury, shortly after their arrival, there. The accident was a simple one. He just slipped on a high ridge in the fog, and tumbled into a deep gorge. I don't know what to say to all that, except that he financed us all, and looked as though his chances of taking care of himself were better than with most.

Thomas sent photographs of himself. He's not so thin anymore. He can grin. The kid in him is dead. There are photographs of Venus. Think of a cellar full of steam. But sometimes it's snow. Boiling hot. Then cold. That's the climate. The vegetation is low and crusty. It cakes the continents and scums the oceans. The mountains are hidden in the fog. And there are the test stations, to find out what Venus is, was, and will be like. You know how the stations look. It's like everywhere. Low domes, barometers, and wind gauges on top. Cosmic ray testing equipment. And everything inside to study air, soil, rock, water, fauna, flora—what not.

So what is Venus? Twin of the Earth in size. Just a trifle smaller. Should be another, warmer Earth. Only it's not. Instead its a problem world. What can you use it for? The crazy exaggerated seasons, because of the great tilt to the plane of its orbit. The long days. The heavy atmosphere. The place might be more useful if it had no atmosphere at all. And there aren't even any specially valuable mineral deposits.

I'll show you the pictures of Venus when I see you. There are also those of Mercury. Dead as the Moon, but maybe promising someway. For instance, at the center of its forever-sunward side they're building a great solar observatory—shielded against the heat, of course. Like putting up a lot of gauges to keep tabs on the functioning of the central power plant of the solar system is the way Thomas expresses it.

I guess he found himself. Maybe he's no great scientist. But he fits in with planetary research. Strange tough conditions don't bother him. They seem to give him a lift, instead. He'll be okay.

Devlin married Jeanne Pauls, right after you left. I guess you thought it was bad. Maybe it is. And now they've got an heir. I'd say that he's one of the first kids born off of Earth. All right, somebody says that space is too rugged for young love, much less babies. So it happens anyway. And Jeanne, remembering you, says, 'Ask that Gannet what he thinks I thought I wanted from life, anyway, just a new hat?' She's okay.

You know Devlin, the dreamer—the scientific visionary. There's something of the South Seas beachcomber in that guy—and he's brought it out there—in his head. He has done some of the work you are doing. He's brought back a lot of ancient instruments. He's worked in the metals labs of the big refiners. Now he's on his own again. Maybe he'll make out someway. He thinks of things like vacation centers in the Belt—featuring new sports-like races in Pusher equipped space armor, from asteroid to asteroid. I guess maybe stuff like that will happen. Sometime.

Well—enough for now. I hope I'll see you. Norman Glodosky.

So Gannet felt himself stirred up. And it was the same with Harwin.

"I guess the wind blows the other way for us just now, don't it?" Harwin said, and grinned.

"Yep, it does," Gannet agreed. "For now, anyway." He felt the urge in him. Go back to Ceres. Just for a look. For old times. But more for facts unraveling themselves strangely from the unknown. The future becoming the present, and turning itself into the visible and indelible past. Not hidden anymore, but still mysterious.

Harwin still grinned—and it was right that he should. It was no lack of warmth for the memory of Phelps. Flash Phelps. Cocky. Sure. Brave. Opulent.

"You'd say, 'scratch three.' " Harwin commented.

Gannet felt not grief so much as a frosty tingling. Surprise. As if he thought that there should be no end to Phelps, ever.

"And Devlin, the kid we thought was Earthbound, has a son in the Belt," Harwin said further.

"This all needs looking into," Gannet laughed.

They said so long to Roscoe and Lenz. There were even a couple of girls in Refuge to kiss goodbye—for a hundred hours, or for good. Then they picked up and left with the casual ease of tramps, the same as if they were going out for another net load. The meaning, here, might be less or more than this. They went out across the millions of miles. To Ceres.

CHAPTER EIGHT

BoomTown had grown. Weight, under Cerean gravity, put scant limits on its potential for spidery height. For the beacons and guard towers.

But Glodosky wasn't much changed. Steadier and cooler, that was all. Another guy with a niche, now. The three went to a small cluttered apartment in a new building, and looked on the Devlin heir with appropriate and flattering comments, mostly for Jeanne's sake, while they saw nothing new. A red, healthy kid. A young couple struggling. How old a picture was that? And did its being on an asteroid make any difference?

Devlin searched their faces, and they searched his. Catching up on time that was. Then it was more or less as it used to be.

"Do you still mumble?" Harwin asked brashly.

Devlin blushed.

"Sure he does," Jeanne laughed.

Devlin made a mock sour face and said, "Want to see what about?"

He showed them a lot of pieces of apparatus from the ancients. "I'm supposed to take them apart and to try to see what they're for. Or what they're parts of. Sometimes you can assemble pieces into something more complete. I've got a knack for it. Sometimes it's very hard going. The archeological research division, coordinating with the physical research section pays me for data on devices delivered to me. And the same to a lot of other guys. Sometimes it gets a little screwy. For instance this little brush. Does it sound sensible to you that the ancients used such things to oil their leathery hides? It was me that found it out. From a color photograph fifty million years old, half burnt away. Maybe I'll find out sometime if they had advertising. For cosmetic products."

Devlin laughed and went on: "But that brings up another point—their color photography. Fragments of film emulsions have been put under test. That's a job mostly for a big lab. But I did find out one thing about their cameras on my own. They used not lenses of quartz or glass, but of clear gelatin. Focus then is controlled by flattening or thickening the lens—tensile shaping, as in the human eye. I found a little sac of thin plastic in a broken piece of a camera, and dried residue of the gelatin, and figured it out. In other films—surgery, medicine, manufacturing processes, the same hunt goes on. Almost in any subject you can name. Superimposing what they knew on what we know…"

"Some would call that bad, Devlin," Harwin chuckled. "A weakening force. Men should invent their own gadgets, not pirate them."

"And who lives to invent gadgets?" Devlin shot back at him. "I live for fun. And the pay dirt of exploration is richer when you've got more hints to explore. It's more exciting— particularly when the hints come from a world that blew up, leaving enough behind, preserved, perfectly. Nothing like that is true on Mars. Too much weathering in an atmosphere. Nope—there's no place outside the Earth and in the solar system, as wonderful as the Belt."

Just then Devlin sounded sure—convinced. A guy who had jiggled into his own particular place.

"How did the Martians blow up this world?" Gannet asked. "Has that been figured out yet?"

For a second Devlin looked scared—as if the question posed a hidden answer that still might be a danger out here. "You can guess that it was atomic, of course," he said. "Otherwise there's not much data—yet. But forget it. What else have I got to show you? Books on thin sheets of metal, that nobody has read much of yet, you no doubt know. No—let's get back to photography. Lots of guys bring lots of half-burned junk in. And I get the restored prints. I've got quite a collection. Here…"

Gannet hadn't really seen the like, before. Those photos, in color, might have been taken yesterday. High thin clouds, no doubt ice crystals. Deep blue sky, almost like that of

Mars. But the hills and plains were green. Often the vegetation was planted in rows, too. Gannet had walked across such rows, dried out and blackened, on chips of the outer crust of that world. The surface asteroids, they were called.

And in the various pictures, shapes reared up—quasi-human at a distance, leathery, decorated with bright bits of color. There were the many mummies he had seen, filled out, animated again. In some pictures, they bent over strange machines. In others—well there were a great deal of others.

Gannet laughed. "You want to put old machinery together, Devlin," he said. "Why not put the whole planet together again? The pieces are all floating in space. Including all the smallest ones, which can't be seen from Earth, they'd make a world as big as Mars. It would be a real restoration."

"You think you're joshing," Devlin told him with a grin. "I thought of that. It could be done. With a lot of Pushers, the pieces could be collected. Still—what for? The asteroids are better as they are. They make a very special region. Which brings me to something else…"

Devlin spread some plans on a table. "A house," he continued. "A covering of thin, transparent plastic, with an inner layer of gum as a sealer against meteors. A sort of huge tent, covering house and gardens. The life of Riley. It could be nice. Beautiful! It's happening already, Gannet. Permanent colonists, loaded with their junk, are moving in. To farm. To feed the miners. To make things like they were at home. Me—I'm a family man, now. There's got to be a place for kids…"

Gannet felt elation creeping over him. Something like a meaning was—or seemed—much clearer to him now. One civilization creeping over the wreckage of another. Order coming out of chaos. From the murder of colonial beginnings. And the harshness of space. He really felt part of something big. He felt that his life was well spent. But maybe the groundwork was laid, and it was time for a shift. He'd had enough of the lonely thrills of vast distance, and of the danger in it.

He even looked at another kind of photograph—atop a cabinet of books. A girl just emerging from the gangling stage. A brat beginning to bud with great promise.

"I saw her before, Devlin," he said. "Just before we left Earth."

"Yeah, Gannet," Devlin said. "The brat. My sister, Kath... She's crazy. She wants to come here, too." His eyes teased.

Gannet thought of the thousand times that he'd envied Tobias. The guy who had stayed home with his wife. The guy whose choice had been along the path of good sense.

"It happens here, too," he said suddenly. "I'm gonna write to Tobias and his Kitty. I'm gonna put them straight. I wonder how they are. Life in a cottage. With roses. Well— that's a lot, too. I'll write right now..."

Jeanne's expression sobered suddenly. "Don't do it, Gannet," she said.

"Why?"

"Tobias is sick." She touched a finger to her forehead.

Gannet felt the prickles of surprise and strangeness again. "Am I guessing the reason for his sickness?" he asked.

"Probably," Jeanne answered.

Her eyes were soft.

Gannet looked back in time to see Tobias pleading that he was not yellow. While he didn't live up to his own standard. All he had had to do was get rid of those ideas. Relax on Earth. Accept his Kitty's pattern. But he hadn't been able to. He was in an emotional trap. Maybe all people were, partly. You could die in space. But you could die on Earth, too.

"Has his Kitty stuck with him?" Gannet demanded.

"Yes," Jeanne answered.

"If he'd come along with us, he'd probably be both alive and sane," Gannet said.

Devlin's grin was elfin. "Probably," he said.

Gannet and Harwin spent several days on Ceres, loosening up and doing the town. Gannet still meant to stay. But at last Harwin grew bored.

"It's fun for a while," he said. "But I like open space, better. I'd rather be on the pioneering end. Staying in BoomTown—well—what more is it than just another version of what poor Tobias did? No—don't let me influence you, Gannet. Do what you have to or want to."

Harwin was all in one direction. He belonged in his work. Gannet was not so sure. Most of the bunch belonged where they were. After over a year, he was still at loose ends, unsettled. He wanted to team up with Devlin. Maybe it was the idea of not taking too many chances with his neck—and of seeking security. But what had happened to Tobias on the safe Earth sort of disturbed that notion. It was a prop knocked out from under him. And he liked the open regions of the Belt. The strange discoveries. The fun of relaxing in Refuge, after bringing in a profitable net load. It was a way of life that could get into your blood. The adventurer's vanity was in it.

"Got to go wind up things with Roscoe and Lenz," he told Devlin. "But I'll be back—I guess."

They were an hour out of Ceres. They stopped to investigate a large meteor mass, which probably had been examined many times before. It was more or less just whim. The way the sun glinted on flakes of gold. Gannet got out of his ship. He stood on the chunk of gold fleeced wreckage, watching a string of colonists' ships, trailing away toward the farther regions.

Then, all of a sudden, he was very ill. The first thing he thought of was a heart attack. But he knew that that was unlikely. Out of nowhere, and out of a peaceful moment, disaster had come to him. He coughed inside his helmet, and tasted blood in his mouth. Blackness began to creep into his mind. He thought of rumors of the viruses of diseases kept in cold storage like other things, from the time of the ancients, and active again among the colonists. But there had never been any real substantiation of such talk.

Then he heard the racing whir of his air-purifier that settled quickly back to an even hum. He thought of the fluid gum between the double walls of his space armor, that could quickly seal any small puncture, and of course now he knew what had happened.

He thought of the distance, represented by an hour's swift flight back to Ceres. Across cold vacuum. He wondered if he'd ever see the place again. "Harwin!" he called hoarsely, and saw his friend veer his ship toward him as he blacked out...

CHAPTER NINE

IT WAS a long fuzzy pull back toward ready awareness. He smelled hospital smells, and saw the faces of his friends worried around him. But maybe he only dreamed it. It seemed that he was climbing a high hill, and couldn't quite make it. For a while he sank into darkness again.

Then there was Devlin's indulgent voice chuckling:

"You were hit by a meteor, Gannet. It sounds spectacular, doesn't it? A fast stray, from outer space, from outside the Belt. The usual kind—the size of a large grain of sand, and travelling up to twenty-five miles per second. Of course the Medics didn't find it. It went right straight through you from right shoulder to left thigh, and on out into space again. Like a long needle driven in the same course, and producing the same kind of wound—with hardly any time for the heat of friction to burn tissues. You know, don't you?"

Of course he knew! His mind was almost defiant about it. He knew space, didn't he? What did Devlin think?." There were always those tiny meteors. On Earth the gravity drew millions of them into the atmosphere in a day. But the atmosphere there was a shield—they burned up quickly and hurt no one. Here there was none of that. Still, their distribution was thin. If there were fifty to a square mile in a day, rarely would they hit a man. But there were not nearly fifty. The chance of a man being in a particular few cubic feet of space at a given time, to keep a tryst with a meteor from interstellar space, was slim. Yet it had happened before.

"The danger to those hit is seldom large," Devlin went on. "And you know you'll be all right."

Yet if you wanted to, you could say that there was the intervention of Fate in it. Devlin didn't say anything to Gannet about a definite focusing now of the latter's plans. But he must know it was there. It was in his voice. Being ill or injured always swung a person away from rugged living. It was like having your mind made up for you. And Gannet relaxed in this at last. It was time for a shift, anyway. While he was still weak, he began drawing plans. He'd studied architecture at the University hadn't he? Let Harwin, with the pioneer in him, chuckle and go away out into the wilderness.

So Gannet went along with Devlin's idea. They had the funds to start. Gannet had piled up a lot in his year with Harwin. And Devlin, with his job, and with the proceeds of some new processes; and alloys figured out from the relics of the ancients—to which he acquired patent rights on his own—was almost as well heeled, himself. Without getting rich being the main thought, as with Lenz.

"I want a certain mood to what we do," Devlin said. "Otherwise, its the same as with lots of colonists. Bringing the fruits and flowers of Earth out here and growing them…"

Gannet agreed. The rest was rugged work and defiance of space again. They chose an asteroid almost an Earth day out from Ceres. It was a surface chip asteroid, from the old planet. One side held thirty square miles of ancient soil, in which water had been locked through the ages in the form of ice. Most of the latter had not sublimated away even in the dryness of space, after the quick freeze that had followed that vast explosion.

Here, in the negligible gravity they blew up their first great plastic air-bubbles with atmosphere brought out in cylinders from Earth. Each covered acres of the plain, where the rows and stalks of old agriculture showed. The ground thawed, for the plastic roof cut off only the dangerous rays of the distant sun, whose heat was not diminished by great depths of atmosphere, and the greenhouse effect of confined air did its work.

Oh, you kept your weapons close to you. You couldn't tell what might happen, as far out as this. But you kept working. Drilling into the deep subsoil, and introducing heat units to thaw the ice. Then attaching pumps and pumping it into old storage cisterns. A score of such wells they drilled outside of their airdromes. But the cisterns were under the latter. Water was of first importance. For itself, and for the oxygen you could free from it.

It was tough work for just two men and their machines. But it was best that there were just two, whose ideas matched, and who could trust each other.

In the warm, thawed ground, strange vegetation, shaggy and dark green, began to sprout, proving the fact of suspended animation in the frozen cold, and through the ages—at least in the case of certain seeds. But they added Earthly grass. They planted young trees. They planted vegetables. Vegetation around them would keep the air fresh, charged with oxygen for them to breathe.

Then, using the rectangular blocks of stone from the ruins, they began to build Devlin's house; but the more interesting ruins, the more complete ones, they did not disturb. Those with the strange cells and passages that humans could not use.

It was Devlin's house that they built first, for Devlin had a wife and son waiting on Ceres.

Gannet had not bitten off that much to chew. He was aware of being smarter than that. It was in his grin.

To Devlin's joshing he had quick answers. "Right now I'm in this to help you, and for the profit of business, and for fun," he said. By fun he probably meant seeing something blossom out under his fingers. Something that meant that space was really being colonized. And not in a half-scientific and a half-haphazard way. Like rough and lusty Refuge, with its banks, foundries, and trading places.

But it wasn't to be said that he didn't think of the future. All in proper order. It wasn't to he said that he didn't think of Kath Devlin's picture. Kath who was still in high school, on Earth. Or of the girls of Refuge, even.

Devlin's wife and infant son, David, came out as soon as Devlin's house was finished. Then, long before Gannet's first house was finished, he had a dozen prospective buyers—men who had made good among the asteroids, and could pay the fantastic prices prevalent there.

Too bad that no one knew what lay in the ground of this asteroid. A thing made on Mars. A dangerous thing.

Devlin and Gannet expanded their house-building operations. They also admitted people to build for themselves—to set up shops, and residences, and metal refineries, as in other places. But they retained strings of control. Their plan must be followed. There must be beauty, and not disorder. The commerce must be hidden. The mellow feeling of a countryside in summer must be preserved.

SO THAT was their life for six years. By that time their asteroid was populous, and shaggy green, under its many connected domes. There had been a dozen times when Gannet and Devlin, and those who had joined them, had to drive off bands of space hopping marauders. But the result was being achieved.

They had a central lake, a great park, rich farmlands, and a thousand houses, perched sometimes at fantastic angles on weird crags, for gravitational force—what there was of it was always toward the asteroid's center of gravity, while it was not round. Going straight out toward either end of it, was always up hill.

Glodosky came out with the clinic. He was a physician now, having completed his studies in a university branch attached to the hospital on Ceres. To this record, he had already added important research work.

And Kath Devlin came out from Earth. One of the first things Gannet said to her, was: "Miss Devlin—you'll be disappointed here, now. The setup is too easy. You'd like to build from scratch. It's in your eyes…"

She was bronzed and beautiful. Let's see. She'd be about twenty, now. She liked blue. And he had meant what he said. She had all of Jeanne's courage. But she was a finer drawn type. She was here to work in the clinic.

Her eyes smiled as they went over him with that kind of searching that told him that she had heard a lot about him from her brother.

"Maybe you're right, Gannet," she said. "But the building goes on for a long time, doesn't it?"

She called him Gannet without explanation or apology, as if it were what she was used to. And what he said to himself was that here in her was his future...

When the asteroid tumbled over, turning like a pivoted chip in its regular twenty-two hour period, and it was night, he held, her hand. He told her how long he had thought about her—since the day he'd left Earth. And she said, "This seems to be the way it's supposed to be—Norb. Yes—I know your name is Norbert. I thought about you, too..."

It was pretty well settled, then. Though he didn't want to hurry her. She might not want that. Meantime Glodosky developed a crush. He worked with her all day, on local people, and on people moving among the asteroids. Mostly it was that kind of hangdog crush. Common out here. Women still were not plentiful.

Maybe Kath was just flattered. "He talks about the farther planets. The giants. And little Pluto—little by comparison, way out in the cold and the gloom. The satellites of Jupiter have already been reached, haven't they? I guess that was natural, wasn't it? But the others are so much farther. I hear that an expedition to Saturn didn't come back. Considering that the Rings are composed of meteors, I guess dangerous strays must be plentiful there, too. But what will anyone do with Saturn's satellites? Or the farther Planets? They're all so big and cold? Of course I know my brother has found something. Still—well—nobody's tried yet for farther than Saturn, though the Harmon Jet is perfectly good for the greater distances. He talks about going, Norb..."

Kath's eyes were warm. Right then Gannet would have liked to poke Glodosky in the nose. Glodosky's crush was perfectly evident to anyone who saw him within half a mile of Kath.

But there came a moment when all this seemed unimportant. It was while some underground storehouses were being dug. Part of a rusted steel cylinder began to be uncovered. Gannet didn't even know it had happened.

Yet he did remember those last minutes very clearly, later. Walking in the late afternoon with Kath. Walking, or rather gliding. You could swim up through the air, if you wanted to. A couple of small boys were doing just that, nearby. Tussling and yelling.

CHAPTER TEN

Then the explosion came. An eye-searching blop of light. A delayed but terrific concussion that knocked them prone. Out toward the farther end of the asteroid. The ground opened and turned to dazzling fire, right in the middle of a bunch of air bubbles.

Gannet could guess what it was. "An old bomb," he yelled. He knew of course that it couldn't be anything like the giant that had destroyed the planet, perhaps after drilling to its core. But a bomb from the same conflict. A dud, before...

There was no time to speculate on such matters, now. There was just the rush to help. With Kath. Ten hours later, they and the other people were still laboring like demons, sweating, burned by radiation. Five hundred people were dead. A third of the populated area was wiped out. It was not news to Gannet or Kath to see charred bodies, of adults and infants. That had been part of the war. But experience did not diminish horror. Two hundred people were injured. Most of them not badly. For that was the nature of the bomb. It either incinerated its victims completely, or left them all but untouched outside of its zone of action.

There was one exception. Glodosky. He whom circumstance seemed always to have conspired against. He was not at the clinic. Which was left untouched. He was off duty, and on a minor errand. He would have been crisped by the blast, except for those mechanical legs of his. They kept walking after he had all but lost consciousness. They walked him out of the zone of intense heat, before the latter, combined with the airlessness after a dome collapsed, could have full effect. And so spacesuited men picked him up. He was black from head to foot. His clothing was burned off, and his skin. His lungs were seared inside. His body was ripped open. His lips, ears, and eyes were burned away.

Kath Devlin was in on what was done to him afterwards. There were tears in her eyes when she told Gannet, later.

"His legs and one hand were artificial already, Norb," she told Gannet at the clinic. "The rest was really just the same. It was a thing he'd worked on, himself. Make the whole body artificial. Except the brain—which was all that could be salvaged. Put the latter in a case of nourishing fluid, kept warm. Blood is purified, re-oxygenated, supplied with food. An apparatus to do all that can be self-contained, compact, atom powered—operating for months without attention. Then all you do is hook the neuronic contacts to the outlet nerves of the brain—motor and sensory. Then the brain can control and live by a robot form. That is what will be done, Norb. It will take time to set everything up, and hook it together. Wonderful, eh? And scientific and horrible!"

She began to cry. Gannet patted her shoulder. He didn't feel that he should take her in his arms. Not remembering how Glodosky had felt about her.

He got busy with the salvage and reconstruction work, making sure there were no more dangerous unknowns in the bulk of the asteroid, by means of delicate radar. It was an oversight on the parts of many besides himself that among the asteroids such precautions had hitherto been neglected. He got busy with salvage and reconstruction because it had to be done; and he had to be doing something while he waited.

IT WAS weeks before the doctors began the hookup work on Glodosky's doped brain. His mind was perhaps the first to submit to a complete substitution of mechanical form after an accident. That was what this system of replacement of limbs and organs by mechanical equivalents was for. And here was its acme.

Those doctors were more than doctors—they were artists. Glodosky, lying in a bed, at last looked almost as he had been—a squat young man with broad, irregular features, and sandy hair—of glass-fibre, now. There would be no shock of horror, or of immediate and obvious loss at awakening. He would not know at first that he had changed at all. That would come on him slowly, when he discovered things about himself—that he did not breathe or eat, for instance. Or that his voice was made by a tympanic buzzer in his throat. He could modulate these tones with his lips and tongue of soft plastic. He could smile if he felt like it. But his plastic eyes could not weep.

Once he muttered in his sleep.

"Did the Devlins get out of danger? And Gannet? And Kath? Kath! Kath honey…"

Gannet and Kath were among those who heard and winced.

Glodosky was awake a moment later. He felt of his body, looked unbelieving. "Why," he stammered. "I'm like I was… How can it be?" Then his expression turned sheepish—almost embarrassed at his optimism. "No—of course not," he went on. "It's just that good…I ought to know, shouldn't I? Anyway I couldn't have gotten through what I remember, all in one piece. Hell, though—it's a fine job… Hi, folks! Hello, Kath…" He even smiled a little, before the reaction came. His face contorted, and a scratchy sob came out of him.

A physician pressed a bulb. A sedative went into the blood that fed Glodosky's brain. "He has a grasp of things as they are," the doctor said. "With that kind of reaction, he'll adjust. Let him sleep some more."

Glodosky sold himself a purpose the next day. That is, he did so for Gannet to hear. "I had a funny idea that something like this might happen to me," he said. "And there are big advantages. I don't need to breathe air. My body will never suffer from cold. I don't need food or outside water. I'm not nearly as subject to injury as you are. I don't even need a space suit. I could last as long as my brain does. So I'm getting a ship and see if I can reach the farthest planets. Go down into the ammonia and methane blizzards of Uranus, maybe. Where a man of flesh and blood would have a tough time. Maybe the jinx is busted for good this time, Gannet. That nameless thing that statistical science recognizes…that some people are prone to accidents."

Glodosky looked actually eager. He had lost most of being a man. Physical love was out of his reach. Yet he had become a little like a minor deity. But you couldn't probe into his mind. Gannet was among those who saw him wave jauntily, several days later, as he fitted with improved Harmon jets. He flashed away on a streamer of blue fire a minute later. So here was another weird finish.

Kath had tears in her eyes again. Gannet burned to take her in his arms, comfort her. But doing that didn't fit, now. He growled and went away—he didn't know entirely why.

He couldn't talk.

Later Kath talked to him. "It always was just you—with me, Norb. Oh, I know how you feel. He's your pal, and he had terrible tuck, and you think he loved me, and though you know there's no sense in it, you can't help but feel its unfair to him…"

"That's part of it, Kath," Gannet admitted. "But its only a detail. The final twist."

Devlin, working to piece together an ancient sunray tower, talked to him, too. "So we had a big accident out here," he said. "A few hundred people were killed. But more than two-thirds of our project is still intact. In history, there have been lots of accidents. How many times, at home, has Vesuvius erupted, and how many times were new cities built up again, afterwards? Maybe that case is even stupid. Vesuvius is a known danger spot. Here it's not like that. We just have to be careful, that's all. So why be down at the mouth?"

Gannet grinned naturally enough. "I'm not down at the mouth, exactly, Devlin," he said. "It's quite a bit different from that…"

He went to the small house he occupied by himself, and tried to think things out. He was bitter a little. Not much. But the drives were out of him. He felt flat and confused. His trouble didn't seem to lie in philosophy, either. Life, to him, was simple and elemental in meaning. To take what came, to go after things, to taste everything, bitter and sweet, to feel that no part of time was an empty plateau.

So far he had accomplished all of that, and expected to accomplish more. Plot—like in a story—was not something he especially looked for, though perhaps it was there. His race he did not glorify especially as a space conquering people. He knew that here it had been antedated, and among the stars there must be millions of other races, as knowing and aggressive, or more so. They spread from world to world. Like a growth of mold. And yet maybe it was magnificent. The thrill was in the doing.

None of these thoughts had changed in him, basically. Yet he was mixed up. Over the wreckage of the far past— the failure of two great races—from Mars and the Old Planet—races that must have lived more or less by the same code he lived by. His own people were spreading, perhaps toward success. He thought of that. And again, of Benrus, the war flier who should have lived; Tobias who had gone mad for denying himself space, and of Phelps, the rich boy, who had achieved the ultimate poverty of death. Then there was Lenz, not especially industrious or clever, but who was rich now, with metal refineries and space ship factories, and what not—rich beyond Croesus' wildest dreams. Then there was Devlin, the sheltered kid who had found another kind of success in a place where it seemed that he could never belong. But he had impressed his inner self on space instead. Making a mood that had a little of the raggedness and charm of the South Seas. Harwin, the soldier, the roustabout, the casual nerveless adventurer, was the only one who was not a surprise, still asteroid-hopping. And Glodosky was the greatest surprise of all, the schlemiel who turned demigod with a sad touch, and hurtled farther out toward the stars than anyone. Who, then, was left out? Thomas. Little Thomas, reported now to be lecturing about Venus and Mercury on Earth. And Roscoe. And, of course, himself.

Gannet saw Roscoe, who came out to see if his friends were all right after the accident, the next day. Roscoe, it seemed was in on the space ship factory deal with Lenz, and was the mainspring of it. According to report. But he didn't say much about it.

"I figure on entering politics, Gannet," he said, grinning. "To, bring better law and order out here. And I got a new hobby—making violins out of wood from the Old Planet. Properly treated, that space-cured wood can give wonderful tone. I've made three fiddles. Wish I'd brought one along. Used to hate music lessons when I was a kid."

This was Roscoe, the football man.

"Ever been back to Earth?" Gannet asked.

"Sure. Twice. Had to buy machinery. Why?"

"Just thinking about it," Gannet answered.

That seemed to be his guiding impulse, now. To go home. To chuck everything. It wasn't that he was bitter or hurt or anything—very much. Just flat and mixed up and fuzzy in his head. He was just twenty-six, now. Good night—was he old and burned out already? No—not exactly. He figured that he could take any kind of luck that came his way. Anything.

He told Kath, rather formally. "I won't promise I'll be back," he said.

She nodded. "I know, Norb," she said to him quietly. "I'll wait and see."

Devlin didn't protest his decision, either. "Lots of folks are drifting back, Gannet," he said. "That'll always happen. I'm glad one way that you're making this trip. Davy'll have a traveling companion. To Earth…"

Gannet turned a startled gaze toward Jeanne. She looked worried.

Davy is six, now," she said.

"We want him to go to school—back home."

It seemed kind of odd to him for a moment—sending a kid away from his mother, so young.

"Oh—break 'em in tough—from the start," he laughed. "Well—I guess it's best."

"Davy won't be much trouble—on the liner, or anywhere," Jeanne said.

Gannet worked two months more on the restoration of his asteroid. He didn't see Kath so often. And whenever he did—well—they weren't exactly cool to each other. Just withdrawn. But they clung to each other tight, at the last moment. Kath didn't go along with her brother and Jeanne, to see him and Davy off from Ceres.

Gannet didn't really begin to get acquainted with the kid until after the big ship was in space. He was a wiry, sun-browned little guy, with sullen lips. Gannet had never had the time to try to know Davy. Now he felt embarrassed by the effort to be friendly. But the kid helped him.

"Are you scared, too, Gannet?" he asked.

"Maybe," Gannet answered. "Of what are you scared?"

"Of the Earth," Davy told him. "Some of the men at home say awful things about it. That its gravity breaks your legs. That its air almost smothers you. That you can drown in the oceans. I'm scared of Mars, too—but not so much…"

The kid's fright of Earth added a new touch to Gannet's inner confusion. For to him it was hard to see how the home planet could scare anyone. Of course the answer was simple; still, it did not help him very much to realize that the asteroids were home to Davy, while Earth was a Great Unknown. Still it remained emotionally, a strange reversal of forces. An elusive thing of viewpoint, beyond reason.

"Some men like to pull the legs of young fellas like you, Davy," Gannet laughed. "Don't listen. Me—I was just the opposite from you. Scared, not of Earth, but of Mars and the asteroids. Maybe I still am—deep down."

CHAPTER ELEVEN

The liner passed Mars without landing. It came down at the Chicago spaceport. Davy was delivered into the care of a young man from his school. Then Gannet was free.

He didn't bother to look the city over much, though it had soared higher and sprawled wider in seven years. Only seven. Not ten, as someone had said long ago, setting a date for a comparing of notes among ten men. But it seemed a naive idea, now. Chicago was fast becoming one of the capitals of a spreading space empire.

Gannet headed far north by train. To an island in a lake. The island had belonged to his father. It was his now. The place had a cut-off feeling. There were no paths except the tiny ones of small animals, under the brush. The trees had many small tangled branches. The shack was half fallen in. Here was the same world of centuries ago. The marsh at one edge of the island couldn't have changed much since the time when only Indians had hunted in it. Mosquitoes swarmed from its summer lushness. Frogs croaked. And an occasional heron swooped up from it with a primordial cry, and a silhouette against the sky that suggested the pterodactyls. All time seemed to linger here, like a static checkpoint.

Gannet puttered with hammer and saw, repairing the shack. He fished. And the weeks went by. And he pondered. Yes, maybe it was time that he was trying to get hold of. Restless, moving time, making its changes. And the summers he'd spent here, long ago, before the war, seemed like a kind of norm or starting-point to him. Space travel had just begun. It hadn't affected average living very much. Other planets still were remote...

Now he would look up into the August sky soon after sunset, and it was much the same as it had been long ago. Mars was red in the southeast. Just a speck. How could you think of that as a world? A place he had been to? Almost died? A desert planet.

Out there, much farther, and not visible at all, was the Asteroid Belt. Much more significant to him, but lost in the distance beyond the deepening blue of the sky, as if it didn't exist. Yet the Devlins were out there. Roscoe. Lenz, Harwin. And Kath, whom he loved. Infinitely farther, if he still existed at all, was a machine with the brain and form of a man. Glodosky it still was called.

Gannet began to see his trouble. Not exhaustion. Not the griefs and troubles that came with success and were part of living. No. Time had been changing things too fast. So there was an emotional indigestion, after too much newness, too many surprises. He was gorged on living. Maybe that was good. He hadn't missed much. But instinct drove you toward a time and place of relaxation, where you could think things out, shake them into their proper order, and grasp the rushing march outward.

He began to see... Still he stayed on the island far into the autumn, going into the nearest town every day for his mail. And finally a message came, printed from signals that crossed space at the speed of light from Ceres.

Dear Gannet: I made it; I'm back. I skimmed along beside Saturn's rings. I was deep in a blizzard of Uranus. And I was clear out to Pluto. Some meteors from a broken comet riddled my ship. One even went through my chest. But I fixed myself up. Pluto is smaller than the Earth—some. I stood on its frozen snow of air and left my tracks on its mountaintops. It's bleak and dark, Gannet. But there could be the sun-towers that Devlin figured out. There is oxygen, and carbon dioxide—congealed, of course. And some of the mountain tops are ice mixed with rock. Thaw Pluto out, and it would be almost a second Earth...

In the message Gannet read Glodosky's elation and triumph, that could compensate for what he had lost. But he read a lot more in the coming years.

He returned to the island and packed. He was a little like Devlin then, mumbling to himself, anticipating in reverie coming moments; small and personal, yet part of a bigness.

"You know I'd be back, Kath. No matter what..."

THE END

If you've enjoyed this book, you will not want to miss these terrific titles…

ARMCHAIR SCI-FI & HORROR DOUBLE NOVELS, $12.95 each

D-61 **THE MAN WHO STOPPED AT NOTHING** by Paul W. Fairman
TEN FROM INFINITY by Ivar Jorgensen

D-62 **WORLDS WITHIN** by Rog Phillips
THE SLAVE by C.M. Kornbluth

D-63 **SECRET OF THE BLACK PLANET** by Milton Lesser
THE OUTCASTS OF SOLAR III by Emmett McDowell

D-64 **WEB OF THE WORLDS** by Harry Harrison and Katherine MacLean
RULE GOLDEN by Damon Knight

D-65 **TEN TO THE STARS** by Raymond Z. Gallun
THE CONQUERORS by David H. Keller, M. D.

D-66 **THE HORDE FROM INFINITY** by Dwight V. Swain
THE DAY THE EARTH FROZE by Gerald Hatch

D-67 **THE WAR OF THE WORLDS** by H. G. Wells
THE TIME MACHINE by H. G. Wells

D-68 **STARCOMBERS** by Edmond Hamilton
THE YEAR WHEN STARDUST FELL by Raymond F. Jones

D-69 **HOCUS-POCUS UNIVERSE** by Jack Williamson
QUEEN OF THE PANTHER WORLD by Berkeley Livingston

D-70 **BATTERING RAMS OF SPACE** by Don Wilcox
DOOMSDAY WING by George H. Smith

ARMCHAIR SCIENCE FICTION & FANTASY CLASSICS, $12.95 each

C-19 **EMPIRE OF JEGGA**
by David V. Reed

C-20 **THE TOMORROW PEOPLE**
by Judith Merril

C-21 **THE MAN FROM YESTERDAY**
by Howard Browne as by Lee Francis

C-22 **THE TIME TRADERS**
by Andre Norton

C-23 **ISLANDS OF SPACE**
by John W. Campbell

C-24 **THE GALAXY PRIMES**
by E. E. "Doc" Smith

THE EARTH INVADED FROM WITHIN!

They called themselves "The Conquerors" and one day they decided to take over a big chunk of the United States. Soon a strange mist began to form over Kentucky, Virginia, West Virginia, Tennessee, and North Carolina—causing all man-made structures to rot. The President and the state governments seemed powerless to stop it. But who were these strange little men who came up out of the earth, wielding a power that could eventually destroy the world!

Only a staunch British anthropologist and two young Americans had any chance of saving humanity from impending doom. Their trail led to moss-covered ruins, underground cities, and torture pits beyond imagination!

CAST OF CHARACTERS

SIR HARRY BRUNTON
He had the best poker face in the British Isles—but would the Conquerors call his bluff?

MALLORY WRIGHT
This young scientist wannabe answered a classified ad that lead him directly into an unknown, alien world.

JIM ORMOND
Strong, good-looking, and always content—so long as he had a high-powered rifle in his hands.

THE PRESIDENT
Things got hot in the oval office when he was informed that a large chunk of the East Coast had fallen under "scientific" siege.

THE DIRECTING INTELLIGENCE
He was the embodiment of super-intelligence and the leader of the Conquerors—and over a thousand years old to boot!

MISS CHARLOTTE CARTER
This strong-willed spinster was given but one choice by the conquerors—a choice no woman should have to make.

JOAN SUMMERS & ANTOINETTE CARTER
Both of these pretty East Coast girls were taken prisoners by the Conquerors. Did a fate worse than death await them?

THE
CONQUERORS

By
DAVID H. KELLER, M. D.

ARMCHAIR FICTION
PO Box 4369, Medford, Oregon   97501-0168

*For more information about Armchair Books and products, visit our
website at…*

www.armchairfiction.com

Or email us at…

armchairfiction@yahoo.com

CHAPTER ONE
First Message

I SUPPOSE you noticed, Mallory, that the radio is out of commission?" said John Ormond to Mallory Wright, who nodded. The men, both bachelors, had become acquainted shortly after their arrival in New York—and the five years which they had spent in the metropolis had been made far more pleasant by this friendship. Mallory was an amateur of the sciences while John, though in reality a customer's man in a broker's office, dreamed of the time when he could become a hunter of large game.

It was a peculiar friendship, depending, as is so often the case, on a complete dissimilarity of tastes. Mallory Wright delighted in science. There was nothing in its many fields of which he did not know at least a little. Born in Philadelphia, raised and educated in the cities of the East, he had never knowingly killed anything except a few flies.

John Ormond, however, who had been raised in the country, enjoyed nothing so much as hunting or fishing. Deprived of much of this sport by his life in New York he had substituted for the reality a dream life of adventure, obtained from literature. He had gradually collected a rather complete assortment of rifles and spent both time and money in target shooting. Thus, he felt that he was prepared for any stroke of luck that might place big game shooting in his way in the future.

Wright had persuaded his sport-loving friend to install a radio and, after a long period of tuition, had taught him to operate it. After having had it in his one-room apartment for three years the most that Ormond could say was that sometimes he could get the stations he wanted and sometimes he could not.

This particular evening, the sixteenth of March, 1933, was one of the times when not even a sputter emanated from the reproducer. Ormond, when his friend had made himself comfortable, went back to the radio question. "Do you think it is out of order again?" he asked.

THE scientist smiled rather dolefully as he replied, "It all depends on what you mean. Mine too is not working tonight. So far as I have been able to learn, neither is any receiving set in the city. There is an extra edition of the *Evening Sun,* featuring the fact that the city's radio service is dead."

"I thought your set was foolproof."

"It is," Wright replied. "Of course I haven't had time to examine it carefully, but all the connections and tubes seem to be in perfect condition. I telephoned Hopkins—you know that longhaired chap who taught me all I know about radio? He says the same thing—his set is dead, yet he can't find out what's wrong with it. He had phoned several of his friends and they are all in the same fix."

"That pleases me." John grinned. "It's no news if a dog bites a man but if a man bites a dog that's different. I suppose, when there are two million radios going all the time in this city that is not considered news. But to have something happen that makes two million radios silent, gets everybody excited and the papers print special editions."

"It really is a serious matter," said Mallory Wright gravely. "The city dweller has become dependent on his radio for his amusement and also for his education. There is nothing wrong at the transmitting stations and, so far as we have been able to determine, nothing wrong with the receiving sets. So the trouble must be in the air. For some reason the air is 'dead' as though it had refused to transmit the waves."

"Good! Then we'll have peace in this apartment house until the trouble is discovered."

"It looks that way. But I don't believe it will be for very long. Right at this minute, while you are wasting your time fooling with a gun that will never come within five thousand miles of an elephant, the greatest scientists of the country are working on the problem. Perhaps by tomorrow a solution will be reached. But it certainly is a peculiar situation."

Wright went over to the radio and carefully examined it. Ormond went on polishing the rifle. From the neighboring Cathedral chimes announced eight o'clock, the hour of the evening service. And, as the great bells ceased and the last echo died away, the radio reproducer started to emit sounds.

Wright moved rapidly to secure the proper amplification and, as the sounds came over more clearly, frowned deeply, then started to take down the message. For, instead of music, or a voice, a message was coming in the International Morse Code.

At last the code message came to an end. Work as he would Wright was unable to revive the receiver. Once again it was "dead." He walked slowly over to the center table and sat down with his notebook under the lamp. For long minutes he sat there and then, taking his fountain pen and a piece of paper, started to transcribe the message.

At last Wright rose and, as though to shake off something, he strode over to the phone and called a number. His voice trembled as he spoke.

"Hello, is that you, Hopkins? Yes! This is Mallory Wright. Did you get that message in code? I got it, too. Started to come over at exactly eight. Can you understand it? No, neither can I.

"What do you suppose? Think someone is trying to kid the whole country? Well, no doubt it will be in all the papers tomorrow. Whoever sent it also killed the air for six hours. Radio is doomed if that sort of thing is possible. I'm going to spend the night here with my friend Ormand. You have his phone number? If you hear anything new let me know."

He turned to his friend. There was no doubt of his excitement. "Hopkins got the same message I did."

"Well, why shouldn't he?" Ormond yawned.

"You don't understand. Hundreds of radio fans in the city, and, for all we know, in the nation, working on their sets and trying to find out what made them go dead. Then, suddenly, at eight o'clock a message comes over in the International Code. Perhaps a thousand other radio hams in New York copied it."

Ormond gave the rifle a final loving rub and placed it back on the rack. Then he walked over to the center of the room, where Wright was looking at his notes.

"Here it is," said Wright. "Just listen to it!"

"Attention. Attention. This is the broadcast station of The Conquerors speaking. All airplanes are commanded to cease operating over the states of Kentucky, Tennessee, West Virginia, Virginia and North Carolina. All pilots disregarding this order do so at their own risk. Further orders will be given to the nations of the world from time to time—all orders being preceded and followed by a four-hour silence."

Said Ormond, "That is the work of a nut. The aviators of this country will pay no more attention to a message of that kind than they would to a command to fly to the Moon and bring back a peck of pickled peppers."

"Undoubtedly you are right," agreed Wright. "It sounds like the work of a lunatic. But there is no reason why a person can't be insane and be powerful at the same time. Whoever is pulling this joke has the ability to kill the air for over four hours, then restore it just long enough to send this message, then kill it again.

"My personal opinion is that he is in earnest. The only other way to look at it is to consider it a clever advertising stunt. Suppose tomorrow one of the radio manufacturers comes out with definite proof that his machines were the only ones working during this silence? How about that? Of course, the government would give him the dickens for doing it; but think of the publicity he would have…"

"Oh, bosh! *Nightmares!* I get that way at times—dream I'm shooting a tiger or thrusting a harpoon into a whale. Forget it and come with me for a glass of beer and a cheese sandwich."

"I'll come but I'm not going to forget it. Something has happened tonight that I feel is going to change the scientific life of this world."

"Fiddle-faddle! Shake yourself out of it! Let's eat and then go around to that new shooting gallery. You ought to practice more. You are positively the worst shot I ever saw."

"And you are the worst scientist."

So the two friends left the apartment to spend the rest of the evening together. Wright shot at innumerable clay ducks and missed most of them—while Ormond amused himself with just breaking off their heads.

Meanwhile, the telegraph and telephone services of the nation were throbbing with frantic messages. From one side of the continent to the other all the scientific experts of the government and the great radio and engineering corporations were conferring with each other. And at the end of all the conferences the best that they could do was to admit that what had taken place during the past twelve hours was totally beyond their comprehension.

CHAPTER TWO
The Air Blockade

THE next morning every newspaper featured the story of the uncanny "killing of the air" and the peculiar message. Practically every large city in the nation had suffered the same interruption of radio service that had been so noticeable in New York City. There seemed to be a unanimous opinion that, in some way, a deranged scientist had obtained control of the "air."

But why he should try to stop travel by air over a few southern states or what he meant in calling himself by such a fantastic name as "The Conquerors" were mysteries that no one was able to solve. The government decided wisely or otherwise to ignore the entire affair so far as any open activity or official comment was concerned—but under cover a dozen of the best operatives of the Secret Service were assigned to work on the case.

On the day following the publication of the message forbidding air travel over the five designated states, aviators who had previously never thought of making an air journey in that portion of the country became convinced that only by disregarding the order could they be happy. Plane after plane from every part of the country was tuned up for the special trip.

Someone had thrown a challenge into the teeth of the finest sportsmen of the nation. The gauntlet was unhesitatingly picked up and before noon of the next day a thousand aces from outside the forbidden territory were preparing to fly over it. That afternoon at least five hundred started.

At the end of another twenty-four hours two facts became widely known. Not a single plane that had attempted to rise from the ground in any of the five states had been able to do so. Not one motor of an airplane could even be started. And every plane that had started to fly from an outside state had been forced to land as soon as it reached the forbidden borders. In every case engine trouble of a peculiar and unusual nature caused a forced descent to earth. Fortunately there had been no fatalities.

Was America to be defeated by a single day of adversity? There were countless air pilots who did not know the meaning of the word defeat, who simply started to overhaul their airplanes and prepare for another flight. This time the attempt was semi-official. The government, at last conscious of a threatening danger, had asked the two greatest aces in the country to make the Washington-Richmond flight in a government plane.

A happy circumstance had placed Colonel Landry and Lieutenant Murphy in Washington together on the day when the challenge was hurled at the nation. Early the next day they were to take a government hydroplane and start from the Potomac basin. They were advised to attain an altitude of at least ten thousand feet, then turn south over Virginia. If they were able to reach Richmond they were to return at once to Washington.

This was the supreme test—a hydroplane running as perfectly as mechanical skill could tune it, with two of the greatest pilots that the country had ever developed. A start on the river and no effort made to cross to Virginia until a height of ten thousand feet was reached.

The start was perfect. The great mechanical seagull rose majestically in the air and became smaller and smaller as it circled over Washington, its white wings glittering in the sunlight. Then when it was almost a speck of dust it started south on its defiant flight.

The end came all too soon. Those on the ground who were watching through high-powered glasses and others, who had sensitive detectors listening for the sound of the motors, must have blanched when the seagull faltered and volplaned down, seeking safety on the open body of water.

"We have nothing to say," was the terse statement of Landry, as he stepped ashore. The two aviators took a government car and started back to the capital. Soon they were in conference with the Secretary of War, the head of the Air Service and several of the scientific leaders in the progress of American aviation. Colonel Landry, as spokesman for the two aces, made a short and pithy report.

"We had no trouble in leaving the water," he said. "The old boat acted just as fine as anyone could expect. We followed orders to the letter. The engine was going perfectly in every way. We watched the Potomac below and, a few seconds after we passed over the Virginia border, the engine stopped. We started to glide down through the air and by careful handling made the river again. I have no idea what happened but I do know that it never happened to me before."

"Have either of you any idea as to possible methods of investigation?" asked the Secretary of War.

The two aces could only look at each other.

BUT the next day at four P.M., Eastern Standard Time, radio communications ceased throughout the United States. Other nations, such as Mexico and Canada, were also affected. European countries could receive waves originating within their own boundaries but could neither send radio signals to North America nor receive from that part of the world.

The message came, promptly at eight, and this time the minds of the greatest men of America were focused on it. The President and his cabinet had gathered together. In Cambridge, Schenectady, New York, Pittsburgh and

Washington, men who had become famous in the world of electrical research gathered to help each other to the instant solution of any problem that might arise. Then the message came, again in International Code.

A radio expert took it down as it came, and read it to the President and his official advisors:

"Attention. Attention. This is the broadcast station of The Conquerors speaking. Our former order in regard to airplanes has been disregarded. If this continues we will be forced to kill all pilots trying to use the restricted territory and also suspend all use of electric power in these states."

The President of the United States and his cabinet listened quietly as this message was read to them. As the radio expert ceased speaking a hush, a stillness as of death, fell over the group of men assembled around the table in the executive office.

At last the President said, "Gentlemen, it seems that the nation is faced with an unknown danger from an unseen enemy. We have first been prohibited the free use of the air over five of our states. Our effort to defy this order has resulted in the threat of death to any of our pilots and a most peculiar statement that all use of power may be prevented in these five states. I think that we ought to communicate with the governors of these five states and assure them that the entire resources of the nation are at their command.

"Then we should at once offer a reward for the apprehension of the person or persons responsible, or for information that will make it possible. I believe it should be at least a million dollars. If you have no objection I will request the five governors to issue a joint proclamation, offering such a reward and, if the time comes when it is claimed, we will ask that it be repaid by congressional appropriation."

At this point the conversation was interrupted by an urgent message for the Secretary of War. He read it with interest and then asked for the attention of the cabinet.

"This is serious news, gentlemen," he said. "It seems that Colonel Landry and Lieutenant Murphy returned at once to Newport News after they made their verbal report to me and had their seaplane overhauled. Immediately after this second message came they went to the hydroplane and started out over the ocean, determined to prove to the world they were not afraid of the threat of an insane criminal.

"When they turned back and were well over the land their gas tanks exploded and they dropped to their deaths in flames. This message informing me of the deaths was telephoned by the commanding officer at Newport News. It seems as though the threat was more than an idle boast."

"It may have been a mere coincidence," commented the Secretary of the Interior.

"I hardly think so," said the President. "I think that these are only the first of our casualties."

The next day seven aviators died, trying to fly over the forbidden territory. But this was not the greatest calamity to strike the five states—for every piece of machinery operated by or dependent for its power on electricity ceased to operate. The blow came at six in the morning and left thousands of automobiles stalled, made hundreds of manufacturing plants idle.

There was a great deal of confusion but little congestion even in the large cities. There still remained steam power and in the mountain regions waterpower. But wherever the steam or the water was used to generate electricity it was uselessly operated.

UP to this time the masses in the United States and even in the five states so drastically affected had looked upon the messages and the show of potential power as simply a peculiar form of joke. Aviation, though making tremendous strides, was still looked on as being in the experimental stage.

But when the automobile owners of five states suddenly found at six in the morning that they could not drive their cars, when millions of people were unable to use the telephone, telegraph or electric light, when practically no manufacturing plant in five states could start up because its electrically-driven machinery would not operate—then the "joke" was no longer pleasant.

There was annoyance and confusion but no panic. The morning papers, printed around midnight, had come out as usual. It was apparent that unless some change took place the afternoon papers could not be issued. The joint proclamation, offering one million dollars reward for the arrest, or information leading to the arrest of the criminals, was printed in Washington and rushed by train to the five states for distribution. It was printed in every newspaper throughout the nation.

Within twenty-four hours five thousand communications had been received by the several governors, explaining exactly what had taken place and who was responsible for it. Exactly one hundred percent of these letters were written by cranks. Subsequent developments showed that the offer of a million dollars reward had only added to the work and worry of the governors and had not helped in any way to the final solution of the mystery.

Meanwhile in New York, Mallory Wright and John Ormond spent the larger part of their spare time talking over the affairs of the nation. They were both interested in the idea of a million dollars as the reward for clever detective work.

"I could go elephant hunting on much less!" exclaimed Ormond. "We would go together. You could study the reason why there's so much fever or lightning or so many bugs in Africa or anything else your scientific mind requires for its amusement—and I'll see that any wild animal that tries to eat you is promptly killed. All we have to do to make the dream come true is to find this guy who is raising so much trouble down South and turn him over to the Government."

"That's all," replied Wright. "But how shall we go about it?"

"That's easy. Everybody else has failed because he has thought of the average ordinary things of life in connection with radio or the automobile or airplane. Now with me it's different. I'm not a scientist. All I'm supposed to do is to point a gun accurately and pull the trigger and get my game. So I don't have to look at this in a scientific manner.

"For example, I can say that the Chinese know they can never conquer us by coming over the sea—so they have bored a tunnel through the earth and need these five states to place their camps on. Does that entitle me to the million? I can think up solutions like that as fast as I can talk but there's just one thing wrong with them."

"And what is that?" asked Mallory Wright wearily.

"They are not the right solutions."

The nation waited anxiously for something new to happen. It seemed impossible that this second message should be the last. There had been no resumption of electrical power in the five states. Manufacturing interests were working twenty-four hours a day in the endeavor to make use of steam in some way. Horses, mules and bicycles were pressed into service to replace the useless automobiles.

People met each other on the street and, instead of the usual question concerning health, asked, "When is it going to end?"

The President of the United States felt the entire situation keenly. He realized that citizens of the five restricted states were suffering while those in other states were being only occasionally annoyed by interruption of their radio service. He had thought the reward of a million dollars would bring immediate results. As the days passed without any successful solution of the mystery, he became more and more disturbed.

Troops were in readiness at every strategic point—but what use were marines or soldiers where there was no visible enemy to fight? There was only one thing to do and that was to wait—and waiting under such circumstances was hard, even for a man with the greatest patience.

For over a week no aviator had crashed—for the simple reason that none had tried to fly over the threatened territory. For eight days business in the five states had been at a standstill. During each of these days, the President had tried every possible avenue that would show even a chance of correctly solving the puzzle. And at the end of the week and one day all that he could say was that he was still working.

On the eighth evening his private secretary was called to the phone. It seemed that the person at the other end wanted to see the President that evening at midnight. The secretary explained in dignified but cold language that such an appointment was impossible. He was told that it must be made possible. The secretary hung up the receiver.

In three minutes he was again called to the phone. This time his language was less formal and decidedly warmer. The third time he swore. The President, who was passing into the secretary's office at the moment, asked what was the matter and the secretary related what had happened.

"Allow me to answer him if he calls again," ordered the President. "I don't like to be brusque in turning down a man who is as insistent as that. He may be able to tell me something of importance to the nation."

The telephone rang again; it was the same voice. The speaker wished to see the President at midnight. He had selected that time because he thought that it would be most inconspicuous and his business was of a very confidential nature. Who was he? That would be brought out later on but for the present enough to say that he was an ambassador. Of what country? He would tell that later also. Could he come? Good! He would be there at twelve; he would simply say to the secretary, "I am the expected ambassador."

The President turned to his secretary. "That man will be here at twelve. Wait in the outer office. He will say, 'I am the expected ambassador,' and you will admit him to my private office. After that you may go. I will show him out."

"How about the Secret Service, Sir?"

"I don't want them. I sense this man isn't an assassin. I want you to follow out these instructions to the letter."

At twelve exactly the visitor arrived. He seemed to be a miniature man, hardly larger than a child, with a large head, receding chin, bulging forehead and tiny limbs. A large cape covered most of his body and a peculiarly-shaped hat, which he impudently kept on his head, hid most of his face.

At least, it was difficult for the President to give an adequate description of that face the next day to the Surgeon General. When the visitor sat down in a chair his feet did not come within six inches of the floor. The first impression that he made on the President was that of some harmless crank, escaped from a dime museum.

CHAPTER THREE
A Midnight Conference

HE SPOKE English but with a peculiar accent. It was perfect English, almost *too* perfect. There was something mechanical about it.

"I presume you are the expected ambassador?" asked the President, as he gravely bade his guest be seated.

"I am," was the reply. "I represent the people called, for lack of a better name, 'The Conquerors.'"

"I suspected that. The time of your visit, the secrecy you demanded, everything pointed to the fact that you were in some way connected with the people who call themselves by this peculiar name."

"I will not discuss with you the appropriateness of our name," the little man said with freezing dignity. "I am not here for the sake of debate. The situation, briefly stated, is this—it is necessary for our logical development to have undisputed possession of that part of this country you call Kentucky, Tennessee, West Virginia, Virginia and North Carolina.

"We want the people now living in those five states to move out within three months. We recognize that a nation as populous and proud as the United States will not agree to such a request without evidence on our part that we are able to enforce it. We have amply demonstrated our power. Do you mind turning the shade a little? My eyes are weak and the light bothers them—that's better."

The President finally laughed, a little nervously, then checked himself and resumed the gravity that seemed appropriate for the occasion.

"You will have to admit that this is a most unusual request to make of the head of a country that has a citizenship of nearly one hundred and forty million people."

"That is a matter of the point of view. You are yourself an unusual man, at least far above the average American—so you can realize that I do not speak idly. You will set the date?"

"We cannot do it!" exclaimed the President. "In the territory you ask us to abandon is Mount Vernon, the home of our first President and it also holds the sacred ashes of the Unknown Soldier. If for no other reasons these two would be sufficient to make us, as a people, fight to the last man and the last dollar."

"You speak strangely," said the visitor as though rebuking a child. "You say it is your land but a short time ago you expelled from it the Indians. They took it from the Mound Builders and the Mound Builders took it from others. What is the ownership of the land? Power, and that is all. We have never before cared for this land, because we did not need it. We need the land now, however. Therefore we ask you to vacate it."

The President strove to control his anger. "You imply that the people you represent, wherever they are and whoever they may be, are vastly superior to us in intelligence."

"We are," was the astonishing reply. "We are as superior to your race as you are above the ape or the gorilla."

The President laughed heartily this time. "Now I perceive this is all a huge joke."

"As proof of my statement," continued the little man calmly, "I will simply say that we have studied your language and are able to talk to you. Whereas up to the present time you have been absolutely unable to begin to talk to a monkey. We have learned your code and addressed you over the radio—but I am wasting my time. Will your people get out of these five states willingly or must we drive them out by force?"

"You had better give us a little time. It will be necessary for me to confer with my advisers and perhaps the entire question should be presented to Congress. Suppose you put your demands in writing?"

"All of which means," commented the little stranger, "that you refuse to believe what I have told you. According to your psychology, I am a crank or I am insane. No, I will not place the demands in writing. At three o'clock in the afternoon, Eastern Standard Time, on April 10th, twelve days hence, electric service within the designated area will be resumed for an hour and a half.

"Now, I am going. I took the liberty of parking my air machine on your lawn. Goodnight. I am pleased to see that you made no effort to stop me. That would have resulted only in many deaths among your people."

He slipped down out of the chair and stood on the floor. The President later recalled that only his head appeared above the level of the top of the library table. Then, without further words, the uncanny visitor walked out of the room.

IN A few minutes the President had the Chief of the Secret Service Department in his office for a conference.

"I have just had a caller, Mr. Hopegood," began the President, "and before I forget the details I want to give you his description." He did so, and concluded, "We want that man. He may be a harmless lunatic yet, under present conditions, he is a great menace to the country. Find him and we have the secret of the trouble.

"Then I want you to send a personal messenger to each of the five governors of the states that have been attacked, with this message—'The President wants to see you at once!' Make it urgent. They are to meet here in Washington as soon as they can get here. That is an order."

It was four days before the five governors were able to meet the President and these were four days of anxiety for the Chief Executive. The request of the visitor was so fantastic, so absurd that it was impossible for the President to tell anyone about it until the time came for him to divulge the entire matter to the five leaders of the threatened commonwealths.

"Gentlemen," he said and there was a gravity in his voice that amply showed the pressure and mental distress under which he labored, "I have summoned you here to confer with me on a matter of the greatest importance. It is unnecessary for me to tell you about the peculiar happenings of the last few days. The people or persons back of these attacks on your commonwealths call themselves 'The Conquerors.'

"I have asked you to confer with me over a new development of this affair. I have been in communication with one of these people and he conveyed to me a demand that is so singular and peculiar in every way that I felt I could give no answer until I had taken the five of you into my confidence.

"The demand is that we evacuate the five states within three months—that means we are to remove all of the present population and leave the territory entirely in the control of these people. I told him, the man who called himself an 'Ambassador,' that such a demand was most unusual. He simply said that he presumed we would leave quietly rather than be forcibly ejected.

"At the present time his request seems to be the grandiose gesture of a paranoiac, who believes he has unlimited power. But we must remember that so far he has made every threat good. We shall have, eight days hence, a test of his power, to demonstrate that the strange phenomena are under his control. What is your advice, Governor Bawlding—suppose you start the discussion..."

Bawlding of Virginia stood up. He was one of the few old-time politicians who had retained his power in spite of the great shift in party management. In his frock coat, his low wing collar and polka dot tie, he made an impressive figure. He forgot that he was addressing five men, and put power sufficient to captivate thousands in his reply.

"My State, Virginia, is rightly called 'The Mother of Presidents.' Always she has led in the march of progress, humanities and republicanism. Her soil is still hallowed by the graves of the Revolutionary heroes and the Founding Fathers and cemented by the blood of the devoted brothers, North and South, who perished there in the Great War between the States. We have never yielded to force a foot of soil.

"There is only one answer I can make for my state and that is *we stay!*"

HE SAT down. The other four governors spoke—but all they could do was to repeat, with emphasis on matters of state pride, the defiance of the Virginian.

At last the President replied. "We will do nothing," he said. "That is, practically nothing until April tenth. The Secret Service will in the meantime devote their full strength to the problem. It is possible for the Secretary of War to call sufficient reserves to increase the strength of the regular army by fifty thousand men—so that, at any time you need help I will be able to send you adequate forces.

"In the meantime I think that we six had better keep this entire meeting a secret. I am sure that we can depend on the courageous cooperation of the entire country with the population of your five states—but I do not want to start a panic. If thousands should start to leave at one time there would be a great deal of suffering. I feel that we should simply wait and make these 'Conquerors' show their hands. Keep in touch with me, gentlemen, and consider that the entire resources of the nation are at your disposal."

The conference had hardly ended when the Surgeon General called at the White House and asked for an interview with the President. This was at once granted.

"After your talk with me a few days ago," the Surgeon General said, "I at once started my hunt for a hydrocephalic dwarf. I have located over thirty who seem to be very similar to the man you described to me. I have a list of all of them, their residences and occupations, and it will not be difficult for the Secret Service to investigate them.

"Unfortunately for the theory that's been presented, more than two-thirds of them are inmates of institutions for the feeble-minded and the other third are harmless folk. Not one of them seems to have the required ability to work the slightest part of the damage done in the five affected states."

"What did you say is the name of the disease?" asked the puzzled President.

"I called them hydrocephalic dwarfs. The deformity is caused by a great increase of fluid within the skull and, as a result, the head enlarges, out of proportion to the rest of the body."

"And you think that this man who called on me belongs in that class?"

"It seems so, according to your description."

"Then I think that we had better identify every case which exists in the United States and place them all under closest observation—because this man, if he has the power he pretends to, has already been the cause of great suffering and financial loss that cannot at this time be estimated. It appears absurd to think that one man can work such havoc."

"Perhaps there is more than one?"

"You find that out and you will be worth a million dollars!" exclaimed the President.

CHAPTER FOUR
An Unfortunate Shot

AMONG six men, at least, in the nation the approach of the 10th of April produced a state of acute mental tension. If the dwarf should prove himself to be a member of "The Conquerors" by restoring electric service in the states for an hour and a half, then it was almost certain that "The Conquerors'" threats might be made good.

At three o'clock great shouts went up in the cities of the stricken states. All electrical equipment was found to operate as if nothing had happened. And for an hour and a half the people rejoiced, believing their troubles to be over.

Their consternation was great, however, when at precisely four-thirty the electrical equipment was stopped again and activity in those states ceased as suddenly as it had resumed. A hush of despair swept over their population.

And in six executive offices six men sat back in their executive chairs with the weariness of defeat marking their faces.

On the twentieth of April the "ambassador" again called over the telephone, asking for another conference with the President. This time there was no delay. It was to be held, like the first, at midnight.

But at this meeting all arrangements were in readiness for the capture of the "ambassador." The President was at last persuaded that he must be placed under control and force used to make him tell his secret and give the necessary information concerning his fellow conspirators, if any.

The Surgeon General was instructed to be at the White House, also the Superintendent of the government's Hospital for the Insane, in Washington. A dozen men from the Secret Service were hidden in the room and adjoining offices and a squad of marines was at hand, prepared to answer any calls made of them.

The grounds also were guarded, as a determined effort was to be made to capture the airplane or automobile in which the visitor would come. However, this part of the plan was a failure since the dwarf walked to the front gate of the White House grounds. Here he simply announced himself as the "ambassador" who had an appointment to call on the President at midnight.

As before he walked calmly into the office where the President was waiting for him. Without salutation or introduction of any kind he began, "Have you set a date for the evacuation?"

"I have not. We are going to stay. What are you going to do about it?"

"*Make* them leave! There is no desire on our part to kill large masses of people. We hoped that your intelligence would be sufficient to make you realize that you are opposed by a force superior in every way to your own. You should reconsider the matter."

"No! Our answer is final. And we want you to stay here with us. We are going to examine you. There is a doubt in our mind about your mental health."

The stranger laughed. It was a peculiar unearthly laugh.

"You will have to excuse that attempt at laughter," he said. "None of our race has laughed for centuries. Well, I must be going. I am sorry—"

The President stepped toward him. As he did so the "ambassador" raised his right hand in what seemed a menacing gesture. A shot rang out and the little fellow dropped to the floor.

"Who did that?" exclaimed the President sternly. "The last thing we wanted to do was to hurt this man."

"I did it," said one of the Secret Service agents. "I thought he was going to shoot you and I shot first."

Immediately the two doctors present started to examine the wounded man. A moment's examination was sufficient to show that he was badly hurt but still conscious. He simply looked at the men around him. His cape off, his clothing opened to the bare chest, he looked pitifully childlike.

Examination showed that he had been shot near the heart (the autopsy later was to confirm this) but the liquid pouring from the wound was not red. It was of a peculiar pink, milky consistency. The Surgeon General commented on this fact.

The dying man looked at him. "The ichor of the gods!" he exclaimed. He looked intently at the President and whispered, "Fools! Fools!" His form relaxed. He was dead!

"Too bad—too bad," sighed the President. "A useless killing. Not only that but his information dies with him. At least make a thorough search of his clothing. Perhaps he may have some papers on him that will lead to an identification. I think an autopsy is in order.

"Also I feel that this affair must be kept from the newspapers. It will be worthwhile, gentlemen, to make another check of your list of hydrocephalies in the United States. If one is missing, it may be this man; and that may furnish us a clue as to his identity."

THE commands were carried out by the Secret Service. In two days they were able to report that all of the known hydrocephalic dwarfs were alive and in their usual locations. This was before the report of the pathologists who were making the unusually protracted autopsy. Had the Secret Service waited for that report, they would have realized the uselessness of any search for the identification of the dead "ambassador" as an American resident.

The report, written in ultra-scientific language, was read to the President and his cabinet by Dr. Howell, head of the pathological department of Johns Hopkins University, who had been asked by the Surgeon General to perform a complete autopsy. The President listened patiently to the end of the report, then asked, "Will you please tell us just what this means?"

"It means simply this, gentlemen. The stranger who looked like a hydrocephalic dwarf was really *not* a deformed human being. The autopsy showed definite evidence that what we thought at first were deformities are in his case normalities. *He was not a human being, such as we are!*

"His blood is different. It is pink instead of red and the cellular composition shows differences. His respiratory system, in proportion to his weight, is at least twice the size of the average man's while there is a compensatory shrinking in all his abdominal organs. In fact, his organs of digestion are greatly different from ours. Much simpler in a way, and this may have been more efficient, though we do not know just what his food consisted of.

"His brain is very large. It was not a case of hydrocephalus; but an increase in actual brain tissue which gave him a brain twice as heavy as that of the well-educated man of today. The feet are very small, the muscles of his legs almost shrunken. Yet his hands are very large and the muscles of his fingers highly developed.

"We have not received a final report from the miscroscopist but it is evident that the nervous system connected with the eyes is very highly organized. The lower jaw is small, the teeth almost missing. This does not mean that they had fallen out but rather that he never had many. There are practically no organs of sex."

"Certainly a most peculiar being," commented the President. "How do you scientists explain it?"

"I hesitate to tell you. That very matter of explanation has given us all the greatest concern since the first minute of the autopsy. This is our final conclusion and I am not asking you to believe it in any way.

"For years the anthropologists have felt that the human race has been changing. This man, who was killed in your office is probably an example of what our race will be like a hundred thousand years from now. Certain changes in human anatomy, which we have felt to be taking place, very slowly at the present time, appear to have already taken place in his body."

"But was there only one of them?" asked the President.

"Who can tell? Perhaps a million," was the startling answer.

The President was not a scientist and certainly not an anthropologist. But he had sufficient general education to see the point of the Surgeon General's explanation of the findings of the autopsy. They were, however, so far as he was concerned, just one thing less to worry about.

Late that afternoon he had received a long-distance telephone message from Governor Johnson of North Carolina to the effect that automobile transportation had suddenly been resumed and that all of the manufacturing plants dependent upon electricity had been able to start.

The telephones and telegraph were working normally and, to make a long story short, things were normal in North Carolina. Soon after a similar message came from West Virginia and within an hour the President had received satisfactory messages from all five of the threatened states.

That seemed to solve the problem. Evidently the little dwarf, who called himself the "ambassador" from "The Conquerors," was the sole being responsible for the changes that had caused so much disturbance to the nation. With his death the entire structure had toppled and the menace was removed.

The President regretted his death. It would have been much more satisfactory if the stranger had been captured and questioned.

BUT now that everything was normal again perhaps it was better that the man was dead. Certainly the Secret Service operative was not to blame. In acting as he had he thought that he was saving the President's life, since he had been unable to see clearly just what the man had in his hand.

The next afternoon at four radio service throughout the United States was again interrupted—presumably as a signal that, at eight that night, another message would come through the air. That was, to say the least, very disturbing to the President, as well as those who were in his confidence.

A personal interview with an "ambassador" could be completely hidden from the public. But a radio message in the International Code became at once the property of every newspaper and through them of every reader of the daily press.

As before the President and his cabinet met to receive the message. Promptly on the stroke of eight the code words came tripping through the air. This time the message was longer than before. At last it came to an end and the radio expert who had transcribed it read it slowly and distinctly to the waiting audience.

"Attention. Attention. This is the broadcast station of The Conquerors speaking. The United States, having disregarded our efforts for a peaceful compromise and having killed our ambassador, has created a state of war. We have permitted the resumption of all electrical power in the five affected states, so that their citizens will have ample means of

vacating these lands. Our advice is that they do so at once. Signed, The Conquerors."

Such was the message that was broadcast to all parts of the United States. It was impossible to keep news of such importance from the nation. All editors agreed that something should be done—but none gave any indication of just what they considered that "something" was.

The governors of the five states stood firm. All of them issued proclamations, acknowledging the demand to vacate the land, making vague reference to the source of that demand, and leaving it to each family to decide for itself what it wanted to do.

Every effort was to be made to assist those families who wished to leave but who were unable to do so on account of their impoverished financial condition. The Red Cross offered to help. The National Government set aside a hundred million dollars to cover the emergency. The New England states suggested that their abandoned farms serve as shelter for those who wished to continue a rural life.

A small part of the population moved—the greater number stayed. For a while nothing happened.

Then came the mist.

It arose first in West Virginia and at the end of four days simply covered that state with a blanket of fog. It was a heavy, thick, almost impenetrable, blanket of dampness. And with it came semidarkness. Everything became wet and uncomfortable. Houses, clothing, bedding, furniture, woodwork—all gathered great drops of precipitated moisture.

Life was difficult under such conditions. It seemed hard to breathe. It was impossible to keep dry. Fires in the houses seemed only to make the humidity worse.

From the mountaintops of the state it seemed that all of West Virginia was covered with an ocean of fog, great billowing waves of mist. The level crept higher and higher until the misty ocean overflowed into Virginia, following in great tidal waves the valley of the Potomac and cloaking everything in its gray ugliness. Parts of Maryland were covered. Westward the waves of mist rushed over Tennessee and Kentucky. In less than two weeks the five states and considerable acreage in the adjoining states were completely covered by the heavy wet mantle.

AND that was all! The Government issued bulletins, which indicated that as soon as the wind changed the mist would disappear. It was nothing to be alarmed at. That was all well enough for the experts in Washington to say—but it did not sound so very well to the persons who had been living for three weeks in an atmosphere of dark wet gloom.

There was some fog in the District of Columbia, and at times the cloud of mist extended across the river at Memphis, but, as a general rule, only the five states were affected. To add to the distress of the inhabitants everything started to decay. Houses, furniture, bedding, clothing, food supplies, tools, all seemed literally to rot away. Everything became hard to handle and unpleasant of smell.

Food in abundance was provided by the Red Cross but it soon mildewed and became unfit for use. Metals seemed to rust away as easily as wood or leather decayed. Under this double strain the courage of the people began to crack.

So they began to leave! On foot and in covered wagons and in automobiles of every vintage they took with them their household goods or at least such as were not completely rotted and seemed worth saving.

The state governments did their best to encourage the people to stay in their homes. It was believed that the worst was over and that the mist would soon rise. But by this time no one wanted to believe such news. The residents of these states had been through six, seven, eight weeks of the mist and that was enough.

IT WAS expected that of all the people in the five states, the mountain folk would be the last to leave. For over six generations they had clung to their mountains, looking with disdain on the valley and river folk. What was weather to them? They were accustomed to living out of doors.

But they were not accustomed to fog and mist and a continual cold dampness in the summertime and when this curse descended on them, word was passed from mouth to mouth that the world was near the end and that the mountains were to be cast into the sea. That was Bible! That was the prophecy! When that happened they did not want to be on the heaving mountains. Better be with the rest of their kith and kin.

So the city dwellers, the people accustomed to the discomfort of the crowded beehives, remained in their habitations longer than the mountaineers. But eventually they also left. The states were losing their population by thousands each day. The exodus was on.

Two months passed and then three. The mist grew heavier, if that were possible—but there were now no observers of its devastating effects. Vegetation grew rampant. Ferns, vines, weeds of all description pushed their tall stalks upward. Trees that were young made rapid growth. Old trees decayed and fell as rapidly. Wooden houses almost melted away into their cellars. Structures of brick, stone or cement became covered with mildew and vines that penetrated every crack as though endeavoring to tear the buildings to pieces with their long fingers.

Railroad tracks rotted and rusted. The long white strips of concrete road became covered with moss. In the cities, abandoned skyscrapers thrust their lofty towers to a sky that no longer carried larks or threw down sunshine to strutting pigeons.

Now and then a government observer would make a hurried trip through a special part of the doomed land. One of these men spent three days in Memphis. In his report to the Governor of Tennessee, he said among other things:

I feel that the city of Memphis is doomed. Of course there is a possibility that if the mist clears at once and sufficient funds can be obtained something can be done to restore it to its former greatness. However half of the residential section is already so rotten that it would be dangerous to resume living in the houses. All the business section would require such extensive repair that it is a question as to whether it would not be cheaper to tear everything down and build anew from the ground up.

The amount of insect and reptilian life is astonishing. It is almost impossible to walk without stepping on a small toad or lizard. Flies and mosquitoes make life almost unbearable. And any food left for a few moments becomes covered with white ants.

There are a few cats and dogs in the city. The dogs are ferocious because of the lack of food and they all seem to be in a sickly state.

I do not believe that such animals can survive the climate. During the three days I spent in going over the city I failed to find a single person. The city is without life, absolutely deserted. If the fog keeps up for a year, it is reasonable to believe that the city will rot to the ground.

At the end of six months the fog and mist were still clinging like a living death over the deserted states. The nation had calmly accepted the condition as inevitable and all the resources of the republic were being used to help the fugitives adjust themselves to life in new surroundings. All talk of resistance had stopped.

Exactly six months after the appearance of the mist another message came over the radio. This one was short and absolutely clear on its meaning. In International Code it proclaimed its threat:

"Attention. Attention! This is the broadcast station of The Conquerors speaking. Now that you are out, stay out!"

That made many a red-blooded American angry. But what reply could be made?

CHAPTER FIVE
The Mist Clears

THE mist lasted exactly one year. At the end of that time, it started to clear and in another month atmospheric conditions over the five desolate states were the same as they had been prior to its appearance. Once again the sun shone into the valleys and illuminated the mountains with splendor. The full moon flooded the river valleys and hilltops with silver.

Everything above the earth was the same—only on the ground was there any difference.

The earth everywhere was covered with moss or sunk in slime, the slime of death and decay. Little towns had disappeared. Cities were falling apart. All of the works of man were dropping back into the dust from which they sprang.

Reptiles again ruled the land after a lapse of millions of years.

Since the final message to "stay out," the land had been silent. That message had been given wide distribution throughout the nation. There was now no doubt in the minds of the leaders of the United States that, whoever "The

Conquerors" were, they had in their possession certain scientific powers by which they could enforce their will.

But the nation as a whole could not forget that every inch of the abandoned territory had once been gained at the cost of human life. Now, in a little over a year, five great commonwealths had been abandoned to an unseen and unknown enemy. At the end of that time, the mist had gone as mysteriously as it had come. The five states were now ready for re-occupancy. But there was the threat—"Now that you are out, stay out!"

The President requested the five governors, who still retained nominal office in spite of the fact that they had no people to rule, to issue proclamations, urging the former populaces of the five states not to make any immediate effort to came back to their homes.

On the same day the President called a special session of Congress to consider the ways and means for the rehabilitation of these ruined states. Secretly, he was afraid that Congress would decide to reoccupy the abandoned territory. He felt that such a course would only cause future disturbances, the gravity of which he was unable to even imagine.

In spite of the efforts of the governors, several people went back into the forbidden territory. They simply went in and disappeared. Nothing more was heard from them. One group of scientists was not only well-equipped with radio transmitters and receivers, but also took with them, on spools, many miles of electric wire for telephone service. They also disappeared and sent back no messages. These apparent disasters made the President feel only more keenly the dangers of hasty action in settling the rehabilitation problem.

Congress met. There were patriotic speeches in unusual number. A Tennessean, known among his friends as "The

Black Bull" rose in the House of Representatives and, by a flight of oratory, almost threw that body into a condition of hysteria. Cheers followed his statement that he himself would leave the house at once and personally lead the mountaineers back to their humble homes. Tears flowed freely as he declared that, only under the soil of his native state, could he rest happy until the trumpet called him to appear before the Great White Throne.

After it was all over a representative from West Virginia took him to one side and asked him when they could start back home. The Tennessean sadly said that he would like to go at once but that his business affairs in New York City demanded his presence there for an indefinite period.

AT LAST Congress appointed a joint committee with full authority to act, appropriated a billion dollars for the relief of the expatriates, cancelled the long-unclaimed reward and adjourned. The committee met, organized and adjourned to meet again in three months. It was a beautiful example of the efficiency of republican government.

All this time the world had been watching the unusual course of events with the greatest interest. Several of the nations had attached to the staffs of their legations scientists who had no other function than to write full accounts of the peculiar and unheard-of cataclysm that had fallen, in such an interesting, even though terrible manner, on the nation.

As the Surgeon General of the United States entered his office one day after lunch, he was handed a card. It bore only the name:

HARRY BRUNTON

The Surgeon General searched the files of his memory and quickly identified the name with that of a famous English anthropologist.

"Show Sir Harry into my office," he instructed the aide. The latter withdrew for an instant, and returned, escorting a bronzed man of middle age, whose rugged though not unpleasing features were stamped with the distinction of their wearer.

"Sit down, Sir Harry," said the Surgeon General, greeting the distinguished scientist and explorer. "My time is my own for but a few minutes this afternoon—but it will be a pleasure to learn in what way I may be of service to you."

"My errand," returned the Englishman, "while scientific, is none the less—confidentially—official. This letter from the Prime Minister will vouch for the fact that I am here on behalf of His Britannic Majesty's Government."

"But, my dear sir, if you have a letter like that, you should have gone at once to the President. All-important visitors— you know—just a matter of courtesy. Let me telephone and make an appointment for you."

"I have seen him. He asked me to give you this note."

The Surgeon General tore open the envelope and read in the President's characteristic scrawl, the words:

Dear Bill, I do not know what Sir Harry wants but we have a direct request from the Premier to give him any help in our power. Use your own judgment, but do not embarrass him in any way.

Yours, Charles.

The Surgeon General laughed, tore up the note and turned to his visitor as he said, "The President and I went through preparatory school together. He then studied engineering while I studied medicine. Naturally, we are still close friends and at times his notes to me are anything but diplomatic. Now I am at your service, Sir Harry. What can I do for you?"

"Simply this. Some time ago a mysterious man called on the President and was accidentally killed by a Secret Service man. Am I correct in this statement?"

"Perfectly—though the truth is known to only a few persons."

"After his death an autopsy was performed by Dr. Howell of Baltimore and the results of that examination were reported to the President. Is that correct?"

"Absolutely."

"What I desire is your permission to read the report of the autopsy and, if the bones were preserved, to examine the skeleton."

"May I ask why?"

"Certainly. Our government feels that there must be a definite connection between that body and the very remarkable series of natural phenomena that have been taking place in the east-central part of your southern states."

"But, my dear sir—the things that have taken place in the United States are strictly the business of the United States."

"Of course. But you will realize the situation if we should be threatened with similar events in our Empire."

"That is true," agreed the Surgeon General. "I have one of the three copies of that report in my safe; I will let you see it and you may copy any portion of it that you wish. I will also give you a letter of introduction to Dr. Howell. He has, I believe, preserved parts of the body for further study."

HE went over to a strong safe, opened it, took out the report and handed it to the English visitor, with the suggestion that Sir Harry make himself comfortable and put as much time on it as was necessary.

For the next two hours his visitor read and reread the report. At last he arose and handed the sheaf of papers to the Surgeon General with the simple remark, "By Jove…"

"Odd, isn't it?" asked the American.

"It certainly is. My word! Thank you a thousand times for the courtesy. Now I must travel on to Baltimore. May I have a letter to the man who made this report?"

"I have it ready for you. But I was in hopes that you could dine with me."

"Fine of you to ask me but my time seems to be limited. I will let you send me over in a car, however, and—what say—will you wire over and make an appointment?"

"I'll do that. Howell is a fine chap. By the way, there is something more that might be of interest to you. When that man was shot I commented on the peculiar appearance of the blood. He looked up at me and said, 'The ichor of the gods!' Soon after that he said, 'Fools. Fools!' before he died.

"Ichor, as you of course know better than I, is originally the blood that flowed through the veins of the mythological gods. You read the report of the man's blood. It looked more like pink lemonade than the blood of a human being. I thought you might be interested in that detail."

"Interested? My word! And this man actually called on your President and talked to him?"

"He certainly did. Here is something else—he told the President the first night that his people are as far above the human race in intelligence as we are above the apes. He said that he had learned to talk our language whereas, so far, we could not talk to the apes. That was some argument, wasn't it?"

"It certainly was."

That evening Sir Harry Brunton called on Professor Howell. The professor had suggested that it would be best to meet at the pathological department of the university. The reception accorded the Englishman was a warm one. Dr. Howell, who knew of the man and the wonderful work that he had done in anthropology, was more than glad to talk over the case with him.

"It is a real treat to show you this case, sir," he said. "There are so many features of it that make me realize my own scientific deficiencies. I know what I see in this skeleton and I believe my description of the body is as accurate as any man could have made it—but I do not understand what it all means."

"Let me get to work," was the only request made by the Englishman.

At midnight Dr. Howell served coffee and sandwiches. At five in the morning he served a light breakfast. At ten that morning the Englishman started to walk around the room.

"You people made a serious mistake in killing this man. Dead, his body offers a thousand questions that, living, he might have answered. I am sure of one thing, however— there is not a single evidence of degeneracy here. This is a human being who has gone upward, not downward, from man as we know him today. There is nothing in past ages that will answer these questions. The solution lies in the ages to come. Now I want to know one thing. Have you any more beings like this in America? I mean live ones?"

The American smiled. "Not that we know of. Won't you stay and visit the University? Our classes would be delighted to have you lecture to them."

"No time. This thing is bigger than formal lectures to students. Sorry. Must be going. You'll hear from me again."

CHAPTER SIX
An Unusual Advertisement

MALLORY Wright, in a hurry as usual, rushed into the apartment of his friend, John Ormond. "Say, John," he cried, "didn't you tell me you were born and raised in western Tennessee?"

"I sure was born there," laughed Ormond, who as usual was cleaning a rifle. "Right in the Reelfoot Lake region. I'd have been there yet, only I had to make a living someway—so I came East and got that job in a broker's office."

"Good. Here is an advertisement I bet you are the only man in the city who can answer. Listen…

"Wanted at once. American scientist who knows how to shoot and is acquainted with the region of Tennessee around Reelfoot Lake. Apply in person only at the British Consulate tomorrow at three p.m. Good opening for person qualified."

Ormond looked up in disgust. "You know what kind of a scientist I am? Just about able to tell an atom from an Adam's apple."

"You don't get me at all, John," insisted Wright. "You are not going to answer that advertisement."

"No?"

"*We* are. *We* have what the man at the Consulate wants. *We* know all about the lake.

"*We* can shoot and I am willing to match my general knowledge of science with anyone of my age in the city. Things are not going very well in the laboratory and I quit today. It's hard to work with a man who knows less than you do.

"So I am out of a job and I know how long you will stay with that brokerage if you have a chance to shoot. Let's rush there tomorrow afternoon and be the first in line—only I am sure that there will not be much of a line."

"It's a deal!" shouted Ormond, putting the rifle back in the rack. Then his face clouded again. "But what's the use. This guy don't want to go to Tennessee—all he is going to want is a lot of information. Besides, no one can go there. The government says so."

"Let's see what they want anyway."

The next day they were at the British Consulate an hour early. They looked around the waiting room anxiously but it was empty. It was still empty at three. They walked over to a clerk and stated that they had come in answer to a certain advertisement. They were told that they would be interviewed at once. In a few minutes they were taken into a private office.

"One at a time, gentlemen," said the middle-aged man, sitting at a desk.

"We are both applying for the same position, sir," said Wright.

"But I only want one man."

"We know that—but together we have the necessary qualifications. Separately we won't do at all. So it's both of us or none."

"That's odd. Was there anyone else out there, wanting the position?"

"There didn't seem to be."

"Perhaps the two of you will do. Which of you knows the Reelfoot Lake region?"

"I do," said Ormond. "I was raised on the west shore of the lake. I have hunted and fished a lot over the years and I can shoot. I would rather shoot than eat, and I like to eat."

"I presume that you are not a scientist?"

"Not at all—but my friend is. He knows a little about everything when it comes to that sort of thing. Our idea was to take the position on one salary."

The Englishman lit a cigarette and looked into space. At last he gave his decision. "I believe that you will do. At least it will be worth the trial. Suppose you come around to my hotel tonight and I will tell you just what I have in mind. How about salary?"

"Is it a position or a job?" asked Ormond. "A position pays about a hundred a month—while a good job is worth at least fifty or sixty a week."

"If that is the case we had better call it a job and put the wages at one hundred a week for the two of you with all expenses."

THE two friends left the consulate in a jubilant mood. Once out on the sidewalk Mallory said, "He's asked us to have dinner with him at his hotel. What are we supposed to wear?"

"Why, the very best we have."

"But is that good enough?"

"Certainly it is. That old boy is a real sport. Didn't you hear him say that he wanted people to call him plain Brunton?"

"Yes, he did say that—but perhaps only to make us feel good. I'm going to beat it for the library and see who he really is. I suppose you're going back to dress?"

"Not on your life! I'm going to spend a little while polishing my guns."

At seven-thirty Mallory Wright called for his friend. In spite of all his talk about polishing guns Ormand was clean-shaven and faultlessly dressed in a well-cut tuxedo.

"I have found out about our new boss," exclaimed Wright. "You'd better not call him Brunton. He's one of the most noted anthropologists in the world. His work in Asia was so remarkable that they made him a knight, so he has a 'Sir' dangling in front of his name. The article I read stated that he's wealthy enough to finance all of his own explorations. I'll say he's a real man's man. This is going to give me a chance to learn something about anthropology."

"Listen to me, Mallory," said Ormond, grabbing his friend by the shoulder. "What does the word 'anthropo—' something mean?"

"It's the study of man and his culture at various stages of his development."

"You mean a study of dead men?"

"To some extent. Come on...let's beat it for the hotel."

Rather to their surprise, when they inquired at the desk for Sir Harry Brunton and were ushered up to his rooms, they found him clad in old sport clothes and smoking an even older pipe. He was rather amused to see their dress.

"I thought we would dine up here," he explained. "My word—but you gentlemen put on a lot of side. Now that you have shown me that you have such good clothes, suppose you take off your jackets and make yourselves comfortable. I want to talk to you about our trip in private."

It was not until after the meal had been cleared away and the door locked that the Englishman started his explanation. "I ought to tell you, gentlemen, that I am here as a personal representative of our Foreign Office. Over in London we have been rather disturbed at the way things are going here in the States. At times it seemed to be a world problem rather than merely a local one.

"When I was in Asia hunting bones a few years ago I ran into a Valley of Mist. I wanted to look into it but the natives became panicky and the first thing I knew they had me tied to a pony—they never let me go until we were some hundred miles away. I never could learn just what they were afraid of. But that mist, as I saw it down in the valley, was rather like the description of the mist that caused so much trouble for your people.

"That might have been mere coincidence. But I have found that there is very little in life that happens by chance— almost everything has a reason back of it. Therefore I felt that the same reason was back of both of these natural phenomena. My government has asked me to come over and investigate, which is what I have been doing since landing.

"Perhaps you have heard of the man who was shot in the President's office? No? Well, it really makes no difference, but he was an odd little thing and I was able to obtain some very interesting information in Washington. What I want to do is go to Tennessee and see if I can't find more men like him.

"Perhaps you know that there used to be a lot of activity in the mountains of the Appalachian Range—I mean earthquakes and volcanoes and the like. Not lately but millions of years ago. It's still having little earthquakes now and them but mostly the range is considered a dead one. Then, after a long period of inactivity there was a sudden earthquake in Tennessee in eighteen hundred eleven. A lot of the land just dropped and formed Reelfoot Lake, eighteen miles long and three miles wide and no one knows how deep in places. Everything dropped, prairies, swamps and forests. Is that correct, Mr. Ormond?"

"That's what my father's grandfather said. He was just a boy when it happened and they came to the Reelfoot country not long after."

"Did he have any idea of what caused the trouble?"

"No, not anything more than the rest. As far as we local folks knew, it was just an earthquake."

"There has been another explanation lately," added Mallory Wright. "I took the time to look it up in the library this afternoon. All that region is undermined and honeycombed with enormous caves. There may have been an earthquake, but what also may have happened was that the roof of some of those caves got too thin and dropped, and the hole just filled up with seepage from the Mississippi River."

SAID Brunton, "That is good, Mr. Wright. And that is what happened though even that does not tell all that I want to know. Anyway, I want to go to that lake and for just one reason. I think that somewhere near there we will find traces of other men like this poor fellow who was killed, of the men who are in back of this messy business."

"You mean 'The Conquerors'? exclaimed Wright.

"That is what I mean."

"Do you know the danger?"

"What danger?"

"Didn't you hear the last message—'Now that you are out, stay out?' I understand that all who have gone in since then have been killed."

"Hardly. What we know is this—those who have gone in have not come out again. They have not been heard from. That does not mean they are dead, does it?"

"Why—no—not exactly. They might be—"

"My word…you worked it out for yourself. They might be detained there as prisoners. Anyway the three of us are going in—just the three of us. We are going to sneak in through the back door. I have studied the map rather carefully and my plan is this—we'll go to Missouri, change into some old clothes, buy a rowboat and cross the river so that we'll land near a little old town called Tiptonville. As far as I can make it out on the map, that is between the river and the lake. Do you know the town, Mr. Ormond?"

"Hells bells, yes! I was born there."

"Fine. You will be right at home."

"Just one minute," interrupted Wright. "Once we're at Tiptonville what are we going to do? What can we do, just the three of us?"

"I haven't the least idea," answered the Englishman. "I've been in Tiptonvilles all over the world and I never know what is going to happen or the part I'm to play in events until I get there. So far I've always been able to get back to London. I feel that we're up against bigger game than I've ever hunted before but that doesn't make me change my mind."

"By big game do you mean elephants?" asked Ormond.

"Not exactly. Now, as to the part we are going to take in preparing for this trip. We will each of us take the clothes we wear and enough condensed food to last two weeks. A gun and a brace of revolvers for each of us might be of use. You can suit yourselves about being armed. And I believe that is all."

"No scientific instruments?" asked Wright.

"Absolutely none. I have an idea that we will find scientific equipment that will make our instruments of precision look like children's playthings."

"May I ask just one more question, Sir Harry?" said Wright.

"Certainly."

"Why do you want a scientist and a hunter along with you if you are not going to take any instruments and will not even go armed yourself?"

"For this reason. If we all come back I want a scientist to support my story. If I die you will have the intelligence to tell the world what happened. As for our friend, Ormond, every once in a while I have found it a good idea to have a man in the party who can shoot straight to the mark. I never shoot except as a last resort, but when it has to be done it is very important that the bullet land in the right place. Suppose you lads leave me now. We have much to prepare to leave New York tomorrow."

The very next day the party of three—Sir Harry Brunton, Mallory Wright and John Ormond—left New York for Chicago. There the Englishman spent a few hours between trains, talking with a fellow anthropologist. Several hours later found them in Cairo, Illinois.

There they went to a hotel and when they left it, by the back door, they looked rather like average rivermen. John Ormond had made many suggestions in regard to their clothing and it was he who insisted that they remain in seclusion in their hotel room until they had grown a three days' beard.

Sir Harry protested. "I have been all over the world," he exclaimed, "and I have never missed my daily shave."

"You can't do that and look like my home folks," insisted Ormond. "Some of them never shave, just cut it off once a year with a scissors and use it to stuff their bedticks with. You said you wanted to go to Reelfoot Lake, looking as though you were an old inhabitant coming back for Old Home Week. You can't because you're too intelligent looking, even with a three-day beard on. But you can't shave every day, not around Reelfoot, sir."

From Cairo they went via Lilbourn to New Madrid, where they slept at a cheap hotel on the riverbank. The next night they started to row down the river.

"This here old Mississippi River is a funny old thing," explained Ormond. "Sometimes it's asleep and then at other times it raises hell. We'll row across and at the same time let the current carry us—and by the time we land on the Tennessee shore we'll be just making Tiptonville, for breakfast.

"Ever read *Tom Sawyer*, Mr. Brunton? Oh, the devil! I just can't get the hang of calling you Harry. Tom used to do a lot of work on this old river, and he saved Becky when they were lost in a limestone cave. Twain knew a lot about this region."

Sir Harry stopped long enough to light his pipe, then he picked up the oars again. The three men were taking turns rowing. At last his shift was up and he gave the oars to Wright and started to talk.

"It might interest you to know that I once spent a whole day in that Tom Sawyer cave. Of course it is very small, compared with many others. I like to go through large caves—Mammoth Cave in Kentucky, for example—there is a cave we know practically nothing about.

"There's a newly discovered one down in your great Southwest, another in Virginia. The entire subject has been only partly studied. Men spend years in Arctic explorations while, if they could only be made to realize it, there are just as interesting opportunities right under their feet. Of course, you know that caves were the first homes of mankind?"

"I thought the trees were," said Wright, who was beginning to puff from his unusual exertion at the oars.

"You are right as far as man's ancestors were concerned— but just as soon as he came out of the trees, he hunted shelter and safety in the caves of the earth. I'm going to go to sleep. Wake me when it's my turn to row."

CHAPTER SEVEN
Brunton's Hypothesis

THEY reached the shores of Tennessee just as day was breaking and pulled their boat up on the bank.

"I think it might be best to sit here for a few minutes," explained Sir Harry. "There are some matters that I want to talk to you about. First I want to ask Ormond a question. Is there any part of Reelfoot Lake that is unexplored or that has been shunned by the hunters and fishermen who lived around here?"

"Yes, there is—but how did you know about it?"

"Simply by doing a little thinking. I made up my mind that there ought to be such a place. Now tell us about it."

"Not much to tell. It seems that this lake we're going to, old Reelfoot, was formed overnight. Those who settled round the lake didn't come too close because they never could tell when it would start sinking again.

"But the trappers and fishermen and happy-go-luckies, they saw that there would be lots of easy food and good trapping and they decided to take a chance. Land didn't belong to anyone special then, anymore than it does now. I suppose the proper name for most of the people would be squatters. Give them a pipe, some salt pork, flour, tobacco, a rifle and fishing pole, and they were happy for life!

"But right from the first they were leery of the entire north end of the lake. That was a long time ago and it's hard to tell just how the idea started. But the way it was told me was that men went up there and never came back—and at last it was just naturally felt it wasn't healthy to hang around there.

"Last time I was home visiting I tried to hire some of the best trappers to row me up there and they turned me down flat. But they wouldn't give any reason. I suppose that for over a hundred years there have been parts of the lake that were never visited by any man, white or black."

"And you know where those parts are?"

"Certainly. More than once when I was a boy my pa thrashed me for just bragging that I was going to go there."

"Then that's the part of the lake we're going to. How about a boat?"

"Have to make one, I guess, unless we find a cedar one that hasn't rotted under the mist."

"Any snakes?"

ORMOND grimaced before answering.

"Lots of them. Some called cottonmouths. Big around as your arm and deadly poison."

"Do you think that we had better row up the lake or walk along the shore until we get opposite this unknown part?"

"I don't see how we could walk along the shore. Most of the lake hasn't got a real shore—just swamps and quicksand and deep mud holes. Right at Tiptonville the ground is a little high and dry. If we can get any kind of a boat I'd feel a lot safer on the water than I would trying to walk around the shore."

"That sounds sensible. Now, gentlemen, this is what I have on my mind—I feel that the world is threatened by these people who call themselves 'The Conquerors.' I think that this is just a name that they have taken from our vocabulary because it has a certain impressiveness. They think that by using that word they can scare our race.

"This attack on this section of the States is probably the beginning of an effort to destroy the human race. The time will come when either these unknowns or the peoples we represent will have to disappear. Since they first started to send their messages I have tried to imagine where they are, how many of them exist, just what kind of a social order they form. The so-called 'ambassador' told the President that they are as far above us in their power as we are above the ape. That is a rather horrible to contemplate if it is true.

"I desired to locate them, somewhere on this earth. Most of the earth's surface is rather well known, though of course there are some spots that are imperfectly mapped. Certainly these people could live neither in the sky nor under the water. There is just one place left and that is under the earth—cave dwellers.

"Now, follow my argument—because it is important that we all understand each other. The first message forbade planes from crossing over the territory of five states. Why? There are parts of these five states that are practically inaccessible to the foot of man—but a man in an airplane can see everything.

"The United States was planning to make an air survey of its entire territory. For some reason these strange people did not want it done. So they issued an order forbidding all flights over this territory. They not only refused to allow flights but they made flights impossible.

"Then, as though this was not enough, they determined to have undisputed occupancy of the five states. In making this demand their 'ambassador' was killed. They at once started to drive the inhabitants out with a mist. That mist was like the one I saw in Asia, where people had a deadly fear of it.

"Now, to the east of us is Reelfoot Lake, which was formed overnight in eighteen-hundred eleven. For some reason the squatters, who were afraid of neither God nor the Devil, were afraid of the upper end of that lake. They were still afraid of it when the mist came and they had to leave.

"If they came back they would be doubly fearful. Why? Things happened after the lake formed and something fearful was stamped into the minds of the people—a deep conviction that, up at that end of the lake, there is something that had best be left alone.

"The three of us are going up there—if necessary we are going to live there for a while. I want you to remember that only rarely, in handling people of unusual intelligence, is it necessary to shoot. If you do shoot—do so as fast as you can and shoot to kill. But remember that the great factor of safety is to keep cool. No matter what happens, do not show any surprise. All in the day's work. Is my meaning clear?"

"Do I understand that you are actually going up there to meet these people?" asked Wright.

"Certainly. And I hope that they will find us and make us prisoners. That is one reason why I'm not going armed. Lots of this trouble might have been avoided if that ambassador had not been shot."

"Perhaps it may be necessary to do a little shooting," commented Ormond hopefully. "A shame to bring this big elephant gun along and not get a chance to use it. And I brought along a fine Winchester for Mallory. Aren't you even going to carry a revolver, Sir Harry?"

"Yes, I think I shall. It would be handy in case we meet one of those cottonmouths, and I could use it on you if you call me 'Sir Harry' again. What say we eat a little breakfast?"

IT WAS a silent breakfast—not a silence of depression or even of apprehension but due to the fact that all three of them felt that they were going into an unknown country to face conditions that were perhaps unprecedented in the history of mankind. Theirs was the tension of the runner just before the race, the breathlessness of the soldier a few minutes before the zero hour.

After fighting their way through the underbrush of the riverfront, they at last reached a roadway. Walking was hard, for the moss on the road was in many places over six inches high. At the same time it was better in the road than on the sides. The vegetation was profuse and almost matted on the fields.

"What do you think of those weeds, Wright?" asked Sir Harry.

"They're the tallest I ever saw. Over there is something that looks like bluegrass but it must be at least twelve feet high. And there is golden rod, nearly as high, and some asters with blossoms six inches in diameter. This moss is new to me. How did it ever get a start like this on a hard road?"

"I think that this is all easily explained. Remember the mist—for a year this country was dripping wet all the time. There was no sunshine but there was lots of water. Now there is sunshine and, no doubt, the ground is still soaked. And then it is hot here, almost tropical—exactly ninety while we were eating breakfast.

"Heat, sunshine, water are three partners that are able to make anything grow. I must admit, however, that this moss is peculiar. It seems to have a specific rotting influence on the road. Perhaps it was planted here for that purpose to destroy the road as soon as possible."

"At least there is one thing to be thankful for," added Ormond, "and that is that we decided not to pack much of a load. I was born down here, where men never made mules of themselves. Hope we find a boat."

"Why not throw aside that elephant gun?" asked Sir Harry. "That weighs almost as much as all the rest of your load."

"I would rather throw away the flour and bacon. Might need that gun."

Though the actual distance they walked was only a few miles, it was well past noon before they came to deserted Tiptonville. Ormond silently led the way through the silent street, lined with houses in all states of dissolution. At last he came to a central square.

There he put down his gun, threw his pack off his shoulders and announced, "This is Tiptonville. Shall we have dinner?"

"Not yet," answered Sir Harry. "Better go down to the lake shore."

A few minutes walk took them there. Ormond looked around in astonishment.

"Doesn't look like it did," he said. "I know what's the matter—it's those weeds. Here is the old boat landing all right, and we used to be able to see a lot of clear water in front of us. It was deep a hundred yards offshore. Even if we build a boat we'll have to cut down those cat-tails to get to the water."

"I don't think that we shall have to build a boat!" exclaimed Wright. "My eyes must be sharper than yours. There's a boat waiting for us—over to the left. See it?"

Ormond started over but Sir Harry called him back. "Wait a minute, my lad. My word! How impetuous you Americans are. Could have saved many lives in the last war if you had been willing to wait a minute. We eat now."

Ormond came back, crestfallen.

"I thought you wanted a boat—and now that there *is* one you won't even go and look at it."

Sir Harry didn't reply but merely started in to do his share toward preparing a meal. It was not until the meal was finished and the pipes lit that he started to talk.

"I want you to listen to me. This game we are playing is a sporting proposition, though so far we don't know all the rules. But there is one rule that I want to impress upon you. From now on, whenever you run up against anything unusual, walk around it three times and keep as still as you can. Then go off and think it over before you take definite action.

"We know there are not supposed to be any human beings around here. All one has to do is to walk through this town and see for himself that the place is deserted—not even a cat. Everything dead and decaying and even a macadamized road disintegrating. The lake by the shore is a mass of waterweeds. Any boat left here a year ago would have rotted and sunk in the mist. Yet, here is a boat.

"Did you *look* at that boat? I did. It's tied to a tree and the rope looks as though it was new. Not only has the boat been painted and varnished, it has had all the brass work polished. It shines in the sunlight.

"By the shape of it, as I see from here, it's a power boat. It certainly is not a rowboat or a canoe or dugout of any kind.

I didn't intend to be in too great a hurry in regard to that boat. My word. Do you lads know what I think?"

Ormond replied that he did not have the slightest idea but Wright answered almost eagerly, "You have an idea that this boat was put there for our use?"

"That's a bright lad, Mallory," replied the elder man kindly. "There is only one way to look at that boat and that is to feel that it was put there for our use. Now suppose we follow that line of reasoning—if it was put there for such a purpose the parties who did so knew one thing."

"What was that?" asked Ormond.

"Simply that we were going to come here. They knew that we were headed for Tiptonville. If they knew that, there is a likelihood they knew our plans in New York City. There is something to think about and there is only one possible alternative—that the whole thing is simply a peculiar coincidence. Yet such coincidences are rare in my experience. Suppose we take our things over there, pull it up to shore and take a close look at it?"

WHICH they did—at least they made as careful an examination of the boat as they could without actually touching it. There was no doubt about its being new and behind it was a narrow channel, cut through the weeds to clear water. There were no oars but at the stern, there was something not unlike a small gas engine. Sir Harry turned at last to Ormond.

"What do you think of it, Ormond? You are the sportsman of the party."

For once Ormond deliberated before giving an answer. After ten minutes he gave his opinion.

"That is the most peculiar motor I ever saw. Looks like a gasoline engine but it's different. I can't see how a man could run it. There is a propeller there and of course the engine—

whatever kind it is—that makes the boat go. But it doesn't look right to me."

"Think you could start it?"

"I could try."

"What is your advice, Wright?"

"We understand the boat part and we could make poles or oars. I'm in favor of throwing the rest of the equipment on shore."

"Under ordinary circumstances I would agree with you. I made up my mind a little while ago about this boat. If it was left here for our use—then just as soon as we are in it and start the motor, we shall be taken just where those 'people' want us to go."

"You mean that it's controlled by radio?" asked Wright. By this time he was more than interested.

"My word...you saw through it. Ten years ago that would have had us guessing. But the robot is rather overworked by this time. I think that the idea is to have us sit down in the boat and start it—and then we will be carried automatically to our destination on a radio beam or something like that. Suppose we turn the boat around, start the engine and let it go chugging out to the lake without any passengers? It will be interesting to see what happens."

Acting on this suggestion the three men pulled the boat to the shore and, after a good deal of trouble, started the engine. Off the boat went. The water lane, cut through the mass of weeds, pointed straight out to a body of clear water. Sir Harry followed its course through his binoculars.

"Just as I expected," he finally whispered, almost to himself. Then, putting his glasses away, he looked to the two Americans.

"They turned the boat around out there and now it is on its way back. In some way the people at the head of this business found out that there is no one in the boat. Clever! Mallory, tie the boat up and we'll decide on the next step."

The anthropologist made himself comfortable, covered his face with his hat and apparently went to sleep. At the end of an hour Sir Harry took off his hat and started to talk.

"Just three things to do, lads. We have to make a choice. Either get in the boat and let them decide where we land, take the machinery out and row, or pole the boat or make a boat of our own. What do you think?"

"You decide that, Sir Harry," suggested Ormond.

"Not at all. Wright, how do you look at it?"

"I suppose you think that 'The Conquerors' are back of this, sir?"

"Who else could it be?"

"For the sake of argument let's suppose it is. So far, they have shown no disposition to be bloodthirsty. Of course they drove everyone out with the mist but they did not kill the people. I am sure it would have been as easy to have killed everyone as not.

"Now they must be expecting us—or at least everything looks that way. They want us to come to them since, for some reason, they can't come to us—or don't want to. This looks to me like a test of some kind. I think we ought to get in that boat, start it and see what happens."

Sir Harry reached over and slapped Wright approvingly between the shoulders. "Bravo, Mallory, old chap! That was just the conclusion I had reached but I wanted you to do some independent thinking. Our sending the boat out to the lake without passengers has shown them that we realize the danger—while our going in it when it starts the second time will show that we are willing to face that danger, no matter what it may be. So, if it suits you two, suppose we start out on the trip?"

CHAPTER EIGHT
The Brakes Off

THE party did not have much baggage—consequently, it did not take long to put their possessions in the boat. Then the little craft was turned around and pointed to the open water. With the three adventurers aboard, it started on the journey into an unknown future.

For five miles the boat went up the lake, at times through clear water and at others through narrow channels, twisting and winding so that it was hard to be certain of the points of the compass. All that the three men had to do was to sit still. The propeller steadily drove the boat forward in silence while an unseen electrical hand steered its course.

Ormand watched it all with steadily growing admiration. "I'll have to hand it to the guy that's doing this!" he finally exclaimed. "He couldn't do better if he was an old swamper. This here is the worst part of the lake!"

Sir Harry tapped Ormond's knee to secure his attention. Then he whispered gently, "Just as soon as we reach the part of the lake that nobody wanted to explore or fish I want you to give me a signal. Must be something there to interest us."

"Will do," replied the sportsman. "Any objection to my looking over the gun?"

"Forget that you have one. Watch for landmarks; does anything look familiar to you?"

"In places. We're nearly there. That's what I've been looking for—that tall pine to the right. Pine on right side and little hill on the left, 'Run a line between them,' my pa used to say, 'and if I catch you going past that line I'll whale the life out of you, provided you come home alive, which I doubt.'"

"My word! How odd! Nobody here since eighteen hundred eleven. Perhaps we have the explanation for it there."

He took the glass and gazed steadily up the lake. Then he handed it to Wright. "Looks like a mound or a low crater, right in the middle of the lake with clear water all around it," he remarked. "That corresponds with everything else. Things do not just *happen* in the natural world—they develop.

"It may take a year or ten million years, but it is never spontaneous. Of course, the mist appeared at first to be unprecedented but I have seen the same sort of thing in Asia. When we reach the solution we will probably find that the mist in Asia and the mist in North America were both caused by the same natural forces. If that be true, back of these same forces we will find the same intelligence possessed by the same human beings.

"I call them human beings, because I don't know any more suitable name. That poor chap they killed and dissected in Washington was certainly a man. He was different from ourselves—but what else was he if not a human being?"

As he was talking the boat increased its speed and rapidly approached the edge of the low crater. Nearing this they saw that it rose about twenty feet above the water level. The boat headed for a landing, from which ascended a series of steps to the top of the crater's rim. It slid gently into a close-fitting berth cut out of the hard clay. The motor stopped. "Here we are..." cried Ormond.

"What shall we do now?" asked Wright.

"Let's wait and see what the program is," suggested Sir Harry.

They did not have to wait long. Down the steps came a small peculiarly-shaped man.

"Am I right in assuming that you are Sir Harry Brunton?" he asked in a near-English accent, yet one that to the Oxford-bred Brunton had a rather artificial ring.

"That is my name, sir," was the Englishman's reply.

"And these men are your servants?"

"Hardly that. They are my companions. Allow me to introduce Mr. Mallory Wright, a scientist of no mean attainments, and his friend, Mr. John Ormond, a financier of New York City, who is noted for his ability as a hunter of big game."

The stranger merely glanced at the two men, then turned again to the Englishman. "You are the one we are expecting, Sir Harry. We will allow the other two to return to Tiptonville and live there. Of course they cannot leave this area."

"They have no desire to do so. The three of us stay together. It is flattering to know that you expected me to visit you—but I cannot think of asking my friends to miss the pleasure of the trip after they have come so far. Shall we disembark?"

"No. You will stay in the boat until I find out about these men." And saying that, he turned around, went up the steps and disappeared.

BRUNTON motioned to the two to draw close to him. He whispered, "That is a twin of the man they shot at the White House. Look at the hydrocephalic head, the large forehead, the little chin, small arms, large hands, little legs and feet. Not over four feet high. Look at those eyes when he comes back."

In a little over ten minutes the hydrocephalic dwarf came back. His face was expressionless and he shaded his eyes with his hand as he explained:

"There was a delay. A conference was being held. The final determination is to admit the three of you—if Sir Harry Brunton will assume full responsibility for the acts of the other two. You will follow me up the steps."

The three men started to arrange their packs and left the boat. Up the steps they went to the top of the crater. From the water the crater had looked like a mound of dirt, fifteen to twenty feet above the water edge.

From the top of the rim it was a hole, half a mile wide and interminably deep. The sides went down cleanly. It was a gigantic cylinder, a well so perfect in its roundness and smoothness that it gave the appearance of having been bored by the tools of a Titan.

"My word! *Remarkable!*" exclaimed the Englishman. "I have seen some holes, like the diamond mines in South Africa, but this is really the most perfect example of a boring I have ever viewed. I wonder if there are any bones at the bottom? No one can tell from here how deep it is, but it must be miles."

"Your audible thinking is remarkable," commented the guide.

"Do you find it so?" quickly replied the anthropologist.

"Absolutely. It has caused considerable comment among those who have heard it."

"My word! Yet, I will say this—sometimes I sit and think out loud, sometimes I just sit and think silently and—and then at times I just sit."

The guide looked at him with an odd expressionless face which so far had shown no evidence of interest in anything that had happened. "It would seem," he said, "that you are endeavoring to indulge in what you call humorous language. We do not take pleasure in the action of laughter as you seem to do. That is one of the primitive expressions that we learned to be useless many thousands of years ago.

"A few of us have tried, for purposes of research, to rediscover the method. The one who was killed could laugh so that it sounded very much like the laugh of you Middle-Men. I heard him several times—but I did not like the sound. Besides, there was no necessity for it."

"Why do you call us the Middle-Men?" asked Sir Harry.

"Because you stand between the ape and the truly civilized," was the matter-of-fact answer.

"You interest me. It is all so absorbing in its unusual novelty. Now I am sure that there are bones at the bottom of this hole. Am I right?"

"Partly but not altogether. Your knowledge shows your comparative erudition, which alone makes you interesting to us. Now with regard to the bones—I am asked to show you something. Leave your property here. We will return. Besides, there is no need for you to carry it. Follow me."

They walked behind him for over a thousand yards along a well-beaten path around the top of the crater's edge. The rim was well over fifty yards wide but the hole was so deep in proportion to the depth that it seemed as though they were walking on a knife-edge.

Soon they saw a platform jutting out over the void. Though it was well built and able to bear a hundred times their weight it made the three men almost giddy to walk out on it to the heavy rail that protected the edge. They were now twenty feet away from the edge of the crater, yet they could not see the bottom of the hole. It was lost in impenetrable blackness.

THEY were standing there, holding to the railing, when the guide called their attention to a long wooden chute that started near the platform and projected over the gulf for fifteen feet beyond, ending in a sharp dip.

"What does that look like to you?" he asked.

"The shoot-the-chute at Coney Island," answered Wright.

"It seems to be some kind of a toboggan track," whispered Ormond, his face a ghastly white.

But Sir Harry simply turned and asked, "Is it slippery?"

"It is. We have a purpose in showing you this. Whenever we have visitors we show them this. It is what you call a lesson in life. In a few minutes another Middle-Man will be here. We did not want him to come. You recall we sent a message, warning the Middle-Men to stay out of the forbidden land.

"This man came. We used him as we would. Then he tried to escape though he had been warned of what would be done to him. Now he will serve as a lesson to you servants from New York. I am sure that Sir Harry Brunton does not need the lesson."

"My word! But there is no objection to my watching, even if I do not need it, is there?"

"None at all. Your value to us will be in direct proportion to your ability to understand us. These two with you are of no value to us. They are here simply because you requested it. Here comes the Middle-Man. He moves slowly but he moves. Would you like to talk to him?"

"Fine idea," exclaimed Sir Harry. "He might have a last message or something."

The man came shuffling along the worn path of the crater. He walked as though each foot were weighted down with lead. His face was covered with the grime of months and a matted beard. What garments he had were more rags than clothes. Now and then he turned around and looked behind him and when he did so he cried as though in pain. After an eternity of waiting he dragged himself out upon the platform.

"Are you ready?" asked the guide.

"Yes, yes! Anything is better than that unending torture."

"You go cheerfully, willingly?"

"*No!* Oh—yes, YES! Make them stop it!"

"What are they doing to you, my man?" asked Brunton coldly.

"They stab me with fingers of fire. Look at my back. For months they have driven me with those sparks. See my back?"

And he tore off the few rags that covered him and turned around. His shoulders and back were covered with burns and scars of old injuries, none of them much larger than the head of a pin.

"My word! But you brought it all upon yourself. Why did you not do what they told you to do?"

"I tried to but it was hard and I wanted to get away. I thought it was my duty. I have an education. I owed it to my country to warn them. They played with me like a cat does to a mouse. I was starting to swim the river when the electricity forced me back. Oh! I came back willingly—but who wouldn't when those things were stabbing you all the time?"

"I guess we had better hurry along," interrupted the guide. "You know what you have to do, so do it!" he ordered the trembling wretch.

The man turned around and started to walk to the toboggan. Ten feet away he turned and ran back, throwing himself at Ormond's feet.

"John! *John!* Can't you do something to save me? Don't you know me, John? Don't let them do it to me. Say something, please, say something to save me!"

Ormond looked down at the pleading man, then kicked at him with his heavy shoe. "Get away from me, you tramp! Who do you think I am anyway? What do I care what happens to you? Get out!"

The wretch shrieked and started to run for the chute. He threw himself into it headfirst and shot down it into the gulf below. As his body left the supporting framework he gave a scream, a loud piercing screech that echoed back and across the gulf, and finally died away in the depths below.

"My word!" exclaimed Sir Harry Brunton. "Serves the bounder right. No man should go where he is not wanted. Bones down there? I should say so. Clever idea. No blood. No one to blame but himself. Good riddance."

"It is well that you approve," said the guide. "We will go down now but we will take the escalator. I will go and arrange for your belongings. In the meantime walk around the platform and enjoy the scenery."

He left. Ormond, white as chalk and sweating, was trying hard to fight off a fainting spell. He rubbed his arm about the elbow.

Sir Harry Brunton held him on one side while Wright fanned him with his hat. "Good work, John, my lad," whispered the Englishman. "You remembered. Always remember to do what is expected of you. You were splendid. Tell me, John, how did you know the man? He seemed to know you."

Ormond shut his eyes as he answered, "That was Paul Ormond. He taught in the high school at Tiptonville."

"Ormond?" asked Mallory Wright.

"Yes. He was my brother," cried Ormond, covering his mouth to keep from crying.

CHAPTER NINE
A Questionnaire

IN TEN minutes the guide returned. Following him were some pitiful looking human beings, who carried the packs and impedimenta of the three explorers. On the faces of these beings was the same hopeless forlorn expression, the same cringing fearful look that had characterized the face of Paul Ormond.

With a gesture the guide directed Sir Harry Brunton to follow him, and the rest of the party descended into a metal cage, which dropped slowly down a shaft into the earth. After what seemed an interminable time the elevator stopped, a door opened and the guide without a word walked out, beckoning the three men to follow him. Through long corridors they walked and at last they came into a room that seemed comfortably equipped for living—though all the furnishings were of peculiar shape and construction.

"This is to be your room for the time being," the guide said. "You will find in it all the things to which you have been accustomed above. Over there in this white space set back from the wall is what you would call a television set. At the side you will find a keyboard with one bank of letters in your language.

"If you want to see any special country, city or man, type in the names on this keyboard and press the red button. If you also want to hear what the men imaged there are saying, press the blue button. To discontinue pull forward the lever with the yellow handle.

"Tomorrow morning you will be summoned to a conference. I am sure that you will sleep well. We are leaving all your property with you. But you cannot escape. I will show you."

He walked over to one of the cringing beings who had carried the baggage into the room. The slave looked at him with listless eyes. "What is your number?" he asked softly.

There was no reply. Without a word he extended a tube drawn from a pocket and pointed it at the being with his fingers. There was a crack; electricity seemed to leap from the tube and pierce the cheek of the slave. A bluish mark appeared and there was a cry of pain, piercing in its intensity.

"Now then," the guide repeated, "what is your number?"

"Seven thousand five hundred ninety, sir."

"Show me your tag."

The being held out his hand. A band had been clamped about the wrist and to this band was fastened a metal tag with the number upon it.

"What is your name?"

"Barbara Ward, sir."

"One of those useless women! I forgot there were any of you left. How did you come here?"

"My man and I did not want to leave our home. We stayed and you made us come down here, sir."

"Where is he now?"

"He tried to get away, sir."

"What happened?"

"You made him throw himself down that slippery plank, sir."

"Correct. The next time you are questioned answer at once. Now go back to your level, all of you. Quick!"

He turned to the three men, who had been listening intently to the dialogue, and said, "And that is what happens."

Sir Harry Brunton smiled as he replied, "My word! How the brutes smell! They seem to be a very low order of subhuman."

"You are correct," answered the guide. "Now I will leave you. Keep your watches wound. The conference is set at eight o'clock of your surface time tomorrow morning."

The three watched him leave with bated breath until they were certain that he was really gone. Then they looked at each other. The Englishman was the first to speak:

"I am going to have a bath and shave. No need now for further disguise. Suppose we make ourselves presentable, what say?"

They had hardly finished their toilets when a bell rang, an unseen door on one side of the room opened and a table with food on it rolled slowly into the room.

"Dinner is served. Let us eat," said the Englishman softly. He seemed to be in the best of humor but the two Americans were more than depressed.

"Cheerio, Ormond," exclaimed Sir Harry. "Smile a little."

"I can't—not just now. I don't see how you keep going, Sir Harry."

"That's easy to understand, my lad. I came here to find out some things. I am finding them out. Let us eat and be merry—for tomorrow we will see things hidden from the eyes of Middle-Men and the day after that we will see more things and—"

But Wright finished the sentence for him. "And the day after that we will be driven by those electric sparks to the shoot-the-chutes and that will be the end of learning these things."

"My word! You Americans think of the most frightful things, and I thought that you were buoyant. My supper was a success but you two hardly ate a thing. Have to do better than that. Let us wander over to the typewriter. I feel like an evening of merriment and mirth."

The machine was on a stone table near a white space on the wall of the room. "Let's see little old New York," suggested Wright.

"No!" whispered Ormond intensely. "I couldn't stand to look at Fifth Avenue and Forty-Second Street just now. Sir Harry thinks there is a lot of humor in all this but where I was born and raised we thought a lot of our folks."

Sir Harry pressed the keys of the machine. First he wrote *7590* and then, as an afterthought, *Barbara Ward.* His index finger slowly bore down on the red button on the left side. The room plunged into darkness and the white sheet developed a glow that in a few seconds became a picture.

IT SHOWED a long room, lighted with the same concealed illumination that flooded their room. In two long rows down this room things that had once been men and women were trying to sleep. On a platform at each end sat large monstrosities, in the shape of men, yet bearing a strange resemblance to pieces of machinery.

Their arms were stretched out as though in silent benediction over the sleeping masses. Yet their hands held tubes and now and then cracking sparks of electricity would leap to find a resting place in the bodies of some of the things who had failed to keep a deathlike silence. When this happened, a dog-like howl of terror would come from the stricken prisoner.

Slowly the picture shifted until it focused directly on a woman. Her eyes were open and she breathed rapidly through her mouth—Barbara Ward. Sir Harry pressed the blue button, and a voice came from the woman though her lips hardly moved.

"I can't stand it. I can't stand it. I ought to have ended it long ago. I would have if I had not been such a coward. What is the use of living when there is no hope?"

She raised her right hand. Something glistened in it as the mechanical guard threw down the tormenting sparks on her. She had plunged a piece of sharp metal into her heart. She died without a sound.

The picture went black with her loss of consciousness.

Ormond leaped forward and took the lever with the yellow handle and pulled it forward. The light on the screen faded. The man from Tennessee looked at the Englishman.

"What now?" he asked expectantly.

"Bally fool, that woman!" said Sir Harry. "What did she want to go and kill herself for? Got the floor all bloody, by Jove! Let me get at that machine. I want to see dear old London."

Ormond looked at his friend. Wright winced. Ormond turned, walked over to one of the couches, threw himself on it and turned his face to the wall. He was in the land of the dead for the next eight hours.

For two hours Sir Harry played with the machine. He saw a hundred different places, fifty men he knew. He heard the

President of the United States talk with his Secretary of State. Wright sat on one side, looking on but saying nothing.

At last the yellow lever brought back the lighted room. The Englishman lit his pipe and smoked in an apparently thoughtless manner. At last he spoke.

"Mallory, I want to say something to you. You have seen this machine work tonight. It is evidently very efficient in every way. I want you to keep one thing in mind, my lad. These people like me. Since I met them I have not only been talking their way but thinking their way. Now there is more than one machine like this, dear boy. Try to get John to see that fact—more than *one machine!*

"These people want me here for some reason and they don't want you and John at all, at least not as my companions. I suppose, though, they could use you a while as part of that crowd of rotting humanity. So tell John that perhaps every room has a machine like this and tell him to be as careful of his thoughts as of his words—because I may have a hard time protecting you lads and I don't want anything to happen to you. Now, what say we get some sleep?"

THEY were all up and active by seven the next morning. At seven-thirty the table of food again appeared in the same strange manner, and at ten minutes of eight the guide of the day before returned. He simply beckoned the three to follow him. The course that he took was confusing—through long winding tunnels and up and down elevator shafts in metal cages.

The visitors were relieved when at last he escorted them into a large room and told them to be seated. They had hardly seated themselves on the comfortable chairs when a door opened and through it walked three more dwarfs, similar to their guide but with even larger heads. Without the loss of a minute the three sat down opposite the explorers and the one in the middle began the conversation.

"I understand you are the Middle-Man called Sir Harry Brunton? You need not answer. The question was a mere formality. We are the three Coordinators of our race, ranking next to the Directing Intelligence. We have come here to meet you and to explain the reasons for your being allowed to come to Reelfoot Lake.

"Our nation is a very small one. In all parts of this planet there are somewhat fewer than twenty thousand of us. We are headed by a member who is called the Directing Intelligence. Immediately under him are ourselves, the three Coordinators—the name explains our function in the nation.

"Beneath us are the two hundred Specialists, each of whom is completely equipped educationally to direct operations in his specialty for the benefit of the nation. Under these are a variable number of individuals, whom we call Directors. They are kept quite busy directing our machinery.

"Of course practically all of our manual labor is done by machinery whose operation is controlled by automatic devices, such as our artificial men. A few Middle-Men perform menial services requiring little intelligence.

"Such a simple explanation of the nation will suffice for the time being. The Directing Intelligence lives in the same body for about two thousand years—the three Coordinators for a thousand—each Specialist is worn out by the time he is five hundred years old.

"The Directors live as long as they are useful. Of course, all of us could live much longer than we do. But we find that there is an age of maximum efficiency past which it is not well to let the individual live. Our constant thought is solely for the welfare of the nation.

"At certain times examinations are held among the large group of applicants and successors for all of us are chosen. Then comes a period of from twenty-five to two hundred years of special training of the winners—each winner being trained by the man he is to replace. When the teacher feels that the time is ready for replacement he announces that fact to the Coordinators and the new individual takes the place of the worn-out person.

"Since the nation has no further use for the worn-out unit he is allowed to take a painless lethal gas instead of dragging out a wretched useless existence through a protracted old age. Thus the efficiency of our complete mental machinery is preserved in undiminished strength.

"We have no sickness here and seldom an accident. We are well protected by our mechanical devices. However, a very unfortunate happening took place some time ago. One of our Specialists had made quite a study of the Earth people. He prided himself on the fact that he was able to act in such a way as to imitate their mental behavior—for example he tried to learn to laugh.

"We selected him as the ambassador to the President of the United States and the fools above killed him. We had almost forgotten that there are such things as firearms. Our Specialist in armaments felt very badly about it. So we must make sure that we learn more about races like your own that are far inferior to us but because of your numbers potentially dangerous.

"Therefore we have chosen an anthropologist like yourself, who will be our consultant, as liaison of information between the civilizations of the past and ours. We have conferred with the Directing Intelligence and decided that you should be that person."

"My word! What an honor! In what did he specialize, this poor fellow who was shot?" asked Sir Harry Brunton.

"He was our anthropologist. We have investigated and found that you were the one Middle-Man who seems to have a sufficiently comprehensive grasp of the subject to be of use to us. So when we learned you were coming to visit us we decided to make use of you. You will of course accept. You will find the work interesting, and the companionship with specialists pleasing."

"It is an honor to accept," replied Sir Harry seriously. "I know many anthropologists above who would give a good deal to have the chance. There is just one thing that I have to ask. I am not accustomed to machines doing my work for me. I brought along these two fellows, Wright and Ormond. They are just plain ordinary men but they like me and understand how to look after me. I want them to stay with me."

"We agree to that. After you become accustomed to our machinery, you will find a mechanical body servant a thousand times more capable than these ignorant animals ever could be. But we want you to be mentally and physically at ease. Therefore you may keep them until you no longer need them.

"Now we are going to go and visit the Directing Intelligence. He has held the office for thirteen hundred years and the nation has made some progress under his leadership. He is very desirous to see you, and has a great many questions to ask you. After that you will meet with the specialists and be given all the instruction required for your duties."

"It will be a great honor to see your ruler," said Sir Harry.

"We do not use that word here. That is a word of the Middle-Men that has no meaning with us."

"May I ask the name of your nation?" suddenly asked the anthropologist.

"Our name in our language is *Glow-wahr*—but when we hunted for a word of your Middle-Men to express it, we selected the word 'Conquerors,' " the central coordinator replied.

CHAPTER TEN
The Directing Intelligence

AT ONCE the three coordinators rose and asked Sir Harry to come with them. Wright and Ormond went along, as a matter of course. They realized that their position was a difficult and even a dangerous one—but while they were with the Englishman they were confident of his ability to protect them.

As they walked through the long halls the spokesman of the three coordinators talked freely to Brunton. "The Directing Intelligence," he said, "usually stays in one of our eastern centers. But he made the trip to the Reelfoot Lake hole on purpose to see you as soon as he could. That is most unusual.

"Of course, you are only a Middle-Man but you have gone far in advance of your race. At least, you have specific knowledge that we need—and we are willing to allow you to impart that knowledge to us. The Directing Intelligence will give you a general idea of our race although he is not the specialist in history."

As he spoke, they came into a large room that contained only a central table with five chairs around it. At the head of this table sat a dwarf who was different from the others in no detail except that he had a slightly larger head. He remained seated as the party came in. His face was expressionless.

"I am interested to see that you arrived safely," the Directing Intelligence began in a low voice. "The coordinators have told you the reason why you are here. We want you to supply us with certain information during the period of your usefulness. I know that this invitation has met with your approval.

"I do not say that we are pleased or delighted. Such emotions passed out of our life many thousands of years ago. In fact, as soon as we realized that the emotional states of love, pleasure, hatred, anger, jealousy, fear and passion were a hindrance to our proper development, we took steps to eradicate them from our lives.

"As you know, these emotions are simply the result of secretions from the internal glands. We eliminated these specific glandular functions, as we have done with many other things by a process of selective breeding and embryonic feeding. As a race we are emotionless. We are highly developed and highly efficient intellectual units.

"We have always subordinated the interest of the individual to the better and more worth-while interests of the nation. All this will be more fully explained to you by our specialists. What I am trying to do now is to give you a general view of our life, the life you will live with us."

"I am glad to stay on here with you," said the Englishman simply.

"You should be. You have the honor of being the first Middle-Man who has ever been asked to come to our world. Many have come uninvited and, as you know, they have all stayed. They are useful in a way—though not nearly as capable as machines.

"I will give you a brief account of our race. The historian will supplement it but I want you to get it first from me. As you can readily see, we are human beings like yourself—but more perfectly developed. I cannot tell you when we left the other races of men but it was approximately a hundred thousand years ago. Our complete records show at least eighty thousand years of life separate from other Earthmen.

"We were made into an underground nation by Glomin, a great genius. He had a vision of what life would be on the surface of the earth. He developed the idea that life would be safer, existence more tolerable, the fight for necessities less arduous, if we lived inside the Earth instead of on it.

"There is no doubt that when this man and his followers went under the surface they were similar to the Earthmen of that time. So we have two streams from the same source, one living on and the other below the surface of the Earth. For thousands of years one race of men has lived by brute strength and its emotions—while the other has cultivated the intellect.

"WE CHANGED rapidly. There were no wars to decimate us, no famines to undermine our strength and diseases were soon under our control. Our specialists in medicine and surgery will tell you in detail of the advances we have made. You will find it all very interesting; and, at the same time it will prove to you that our ambassador was right on the whole when he told the President of the United States that our race is as far above the Middle-Men as they are above the ape. You are an exception.

"It may be well to explain to you the reason for some of the events of the last year and a half. We have, in these five American states, several holes such as the one by which you entered at Reelfoot Lake. They are in isolated spots, and we had been able to so terrorize the mountaineers that they were more than willing to leave us alone.

"Your invention of the airplane changed all that. It seemed to us that the only way to preserve this isolation was by a prohibition of air traffic over our territory. At the time when we issued the first edict it was thought that it would be at once obeyed and that there would be no more trouble.

"The antagonism of the United States was not a part of the anticipated program. But there was only one thing to do and that was to clear the territory of you Middle-Men. To do this we used the most sensible method—that of making the territory unfit for you to live in.

"However, we are now ready to extend our plans. I will explain this by saying that, fifty thousand years ago we prepared a definite program, which would give us an opportunity to live out our destiny apart from your race and, at the same time to allow you Middle-Men, within limits, to live yours. The working out of this program has been most interesting and you, as a member of our staff, should be satisfied to live here and study its more intimate details. We will go into that later on. Have you any questions?"

"Several," replied Brunton. "Just how were you able to interfere with the radio waves? What was your method of preventing the planes from flying over the forbidden territory? How do you produce the mist? What general method of living produces your longevity?"

"These are all very appropriate questions. First, all of your so-called modern inventions have been our property for thousands of years. We then undertook successive developments that give us an ability to neutralize the powers that we had discovered.

"We control a force that is able to refract or bend all radio waves so that they converge and are appreciable only at the magnetic poles. I presume you would call it electromagnetic dispersion. By a second process, using ionic attractors of great size placed under the earth, we are able to withdraw electrical force so completely from any territory that all electrical machinery is useless.

"The mist is peculiarly valuable. You commented the other day on the fact that you have seen similar mist in a valley in Asia. That was our formation and we made use of it there for the same purpose that we made use of it here. We wanted the population to withdraw so that we would have complete isolation.

"Of course, you know that the center of the Earth is a molten mass. In a few places this breaks through in the form of volcanoes—but everywhere, if sufficient depth is obtained, intense heat can be observed. We bore holes at regular Intervals until we obtain the requisite temperature and then divert subterranean rivers into these holes.

"Steam in enormous quantities is formed. It rises into the air as steam, high enough to be condensed, and then falls as a mist. Naturally there is a great increase in the temperature, with heavy rainfall and a marked growth of vegetation. However, we add to the destruction by sprinkling over the cities and roads a special powder which has a marked disintegrating effect on iron, stone and cement. We do this from our airplanes.

"What we wanted to do with the territory of these five states was to eliminate all traces of Middle-Men. It is simply an experiment; we wish to see whether it would return to its original condition before you began to waste it, revert completely to a state of nature. In one year we have obtained great success in our work of restoration. I think that in five more years we will have a complete growth of briars and berry bushes over Memphis, Nashville and Richmond.

"NOW, there remains one more question. In regard to our longevity I will tell you that, should we lose sight of the welfare of our nation, it would never be necessary for any of our race to die. The factor we use to determine our life span is our efficiency.

"Our bodies are practically immortal. Our nervous systems, unfortunately, are not. We have a period of maximum mental efficiency and after that there is a slight decline. Centuries ago we determined that to wait for that decline would interfere with the upward progress of the nation.

"We combat disease with our leucocytes—the more white cells in our blood, the better able we are to resist infection. In addition to that we live in natural and artificial caves whose atmosphere has been freed of germs. By a process of natural selection we have changed our blood composition until the white corpuscles far outnumber the red.

"We remain few in number by keeping a careful watch on the growth of the population. Only the best individuals are allowed to live. Examinations are held when necessary and all who are not sufficiently promising are eliminated.

"We have just conducted such an examination. Twenty of our specialists applied to the coordinators for pupils—a group of two thousand was ordered to take the examinations. Each specialist has about one hundred students in training— that is about the average size of a class in our preliminary colleges. Out of these the most brilliant member is selected and the failures are either put to other work or disposed of.

"The disposal ceremony will take place this morning so that you may see it. I am sure that its efficiency will interest you, especially when you compare it with the childish methods of your Middle-Men. You spend time, effort and wealth in educating millions who, even when educated, are unable to serve any useful purpose and must be supported by the nation. You will accompany me now to the place of disposal."

"It will be a valuable opportunity," was the Englishman's answer.

The Directing Intelligence slowly arose from his seat and, side by side with Sir Harry, walked out of the room, followed by the three coordinators. The two Americans went along as a matter of course. They were silent—not even trying to think.

After a short walk and a journey in an elevator the explorers found themselves in a great hall at the end of which was a large platform. On this platform a group of white-robed "hydrocephalies" were waiting and, behind them was another group in white robes, edged with purple. The hall was filled with other dwarfs.

"These are the twenty specialists and their successors," explained the Directing Intelligence. "Specialists always devote a great deal of their time to transmitting their knowledge by personal instruction to their pupils, who will ultimately become their successors. This will be made clearer to you by the ceremony.

"I will ask the Educational Coordinator to take charge of the ceremonies and I will sit down. At times the weight of my head is oppressive and I find it best not to over-exert myself. In fact, I think that shortly it will be necessary for me to take steps to have myself replaced."

One of the coordinators, who up to this time had been silent, now stepped to the edge of the platform. He began his short address.

"Twenty of our specialists have asked for pupils and, out of a class of two thousand, twenty have been selected by competitive examinations. On these twenty, the white robes edged with purple have been placed. It will be their duty to acquire the wisdom of their teachers and even add to it—so that, when the time comes for the retirement of the latter, the pupils will be able to take their places and thus preserve the continuity of our knowledge.

"I am confident that you will prove worthy in every way of the honor placed on your intellectual life. I now ask all to form in a double line on either side of the Lethal Chamber door to salute the two hundred who are to be eliminated from our race."

The Directing Intelligence stood up and took Brunton's arm. They led the way to a door at the end of the hall. On either side the specialists and their new pupils placed themselves. Ormond and Wright stood behind but were well able to see over the heads of the dwarfs in front of them.

From the vast group in the hall rose quietly and in predetermined order those students who had failed to prove the right to live. Without a sound, without even a change of expression, they marched one by one through a door that swung open to receive them and swung slowly back before the next advanced.

CHAPTER ELEVEN
An Initiation

AT LAST they were all gone—two hundred men of this strange race deliberately slaughtered because they had failed to show their intellectual right to live as active members of the Ruling Minds.

Then came a double column of men twenty in number. On one side they were clad in white robes—on the ether side the robes were white, edged with purple. Up to them stepped the Educational Coordinator.

"You specialists have taught your pupils all that you know and, realizing that your mentality is passing the peak of usefulness, have asked for the right to pass through the Lethal Chamber. I will, therefore, ask the pupils to remove their robes."

Twenty of the men did so. Then the orator resumed. "I will now ask your teachers to invest you with their robes.

Slowly the twenty specialists took oft their white robes and invested their former pupils with them. Then the speaker walked to the head of the line.

"As specialists you have served the nation carefully and well. You have added to the general uplift of our nation. In leaving us you will have the consciousness that you have never failed to place the race above the individual. You now have our permission to depart. I will ask the new specialists to take their places with their fellow leaders."

And the twenty naked specialists, who had committed no error save that of yielding to the deterioration of time, one by one stepped through the door of the Lethal Chamber to eternity. They too showed no emotion and went to their deaths without a sound.

The Directing Intelligence turned to Sir Harry Brunton. "Thus," he remarked, "we preserve the intellectual vigor of our nation. I will now have you sent back to your apartment where, this afternoon, you will be visited by our specialist in human biology. Tomorrow you will be taken to see some parts of our nation that will interest you. Now I will leave you."

Soon our three friends were back in their room. Their guide left them alone and a table, well-laden with food, shot as usual through the hole. Ormond looked at Sir Harry Brunton and simply exclaimed, "Well?"

The Englishman smiled back as he muttered, "My word! Bones? I should say so."

Most of that dinner was spent in silence. Not until the end of it were the spirits of the New Yorkers sufficiently revived to permit of conversation. Suddenly Wright said smilingly to Ormond, "We both went through high school and college, didn't we, John?"

"Yes—but you learned something and I just went through."

"We used to think that the professors were severe and that at times they failed to pass men who might have slipped through had they had a little better than even break."

"Yes—life at college was pretty hard at times."

"Well, we just didn't know what it was to study. Graduation day here is somewhat different from what it was when we received our degrees, eh, John?"

Ormond never answered. He just stared in front of him with a set expression on his face. Sir Harry struck into the conversation.

"John, my lad, you must control your emotions. What we have seen is efficiency plus. I know lots of men with whom I went to the university, who should have been handled as these failures were this morning. I like the idea. Why should men live who are unable to make the grade and amount to something?

"These brainy dwarfs are teaching me a lot. I would be false to the best in me if I did not appreciate the wonderful system of life that these gentlemen have evolved through the ages while we have been wasting, murdering each other to satisfy the cravings of our various emotions."

While he was talking a white-robed dwarf came in. He introduced himself, as all these people did, not by a personal name, but by the position that he occupied. The name of the individual was a thing of no importance—what really counted was the work that he did for the nation.

"I am the specialist in applied biology," the dwarf began. "I have been asked to come and tell you something about the origin of life in our race. Applied biology, let me say, is very important to the national existence—for if any of us failed in our work of studying cells, their growth and deterioration, then the battle we have won against nature would be lost.

"A great many centuries ago, perhaps forty thousand years, the then Directing Intelligence made the observation

161

that not all women were satisfactory as sources of propagation. Some were sterile. Others who were fertile and intelligent, did not care to go through the ordeal of childbirth.

"In fact, the more intelligent our women were at the time the fewer children they had, and, of course, as our aim was a constantly growing intelligence, we felt that we could not trust the future of the race in the hands of the children of the ignorant. At the present time I understand that you Middle-Men are facing these very problems.

"In order to secure a proper viewpoint we began to study biologic problems and their solution through the older forms of life—the termite, ant, bee and cockroach. From a study of them we evolved a scheme of perpetuating life that has become very satisfactory in every way.

"Each year we select from a group of five hundred mature young females twenty-five of special intelligence and other high hereditary qualities. These occupy the same relation to our biologic life that the queen bee holds in the hive. The skill of many generations of specialists in embryology, surgery and internal secretions has made our queens able to generate one egg a day, which is at once removed and placed in an incubator.

"These incubators are placed on a carrying belt, which moves in an endless circle through our specially-heated and lighted nurseries. Over twenty thousand filled incubators, holding units in every stage of development, are constantly passing through the testing and sorting rooms. For the actual care, the feeding and the nursing, we have specially-built machines.

THE final sorting is done by my pupil and myself. On us devolves the responsibility of removing those that show signs of being unfit—so that the standards of the nation will be constantly improved. When the sex is determined, most of the females are removed. After birth all the infant units are examined by our specialist in psychology and about half of those are disposed of.

"As the empty incubators are at once sterilized and prepared for more eggs, we have, in spite of the large percentage of discards, an abundance of material for training purposes. The females are kept in their own cavern and are taken out only when they are discarded or to be placed in the queens' cave, which is adjacent to the incubator and nursery houses.

"As you have perhaps observed, for propagation we follow the efficient method of so many of the lower forms of life. However, our sexlessness is more apparent than real. A sexless person, by special feeding and glandular medication, can be made into an efficient male in ten years. The only male who retains his sexual power is the Directing Intelligence. He is the father of all of us.

"The queens are watched carefully, and as soon as there is the slightest sign of deterioration in one she is discarded. By our system of inbreeding we have continued to raise the level of our mental life. The specialist in psychology tells me that the race as a whole has a mental power that is at least fifty percent greater than it was ten thousand years ago.

"The various caves under my direct care are in an inaccessible portion of Asia. We will go there eventually but for the present I will show you various scenes from my department. Suppose you sit in front of this screen?

"Now I will show you the queens' house. At present we have only fifty queens there. Our supply of intelligent females has not been satisfactory lately. For two hundred years we have had difficulty in obtaining females of the best grade. They have no function except the production of ova. Their bodies are very small and their heads also are smaller than ours.

"This is a very uninteresting scene—so we will go on to another. Here we have a section of the incubator room. My assistant is at work, sorting out the weaklings and the surplus females. He is a very brilliant and tireless worker and already his judgment in regard to immature units is slightly better than mine.

"You notice that he holds a lever in his right hand and carefully examines each immaturity as it slowly passes before him on the endless belt. When he finds a discard he presses that lever, the incubator is taken off the belt, the contents discarded, the incubator sterilized and made ready for another egg.

"See! He has discarded one, a potential female. Now the incubator leaves the belt. It is taken to another belt by a machine worker, a door is opened and it is emptied by means of a vacuum cleaner into a tunnel which ends in a pit similar to the one you saw used so efficiently today."

He paused briefly to watch the work of his assistant.

"Of course, you understand that the disposal pits we use at the present time are simply the homes of different races of animals that have disappeared from the surface of the earth. We felt that science demanded that these animals and reptiles be preserved—so we dug these enormous holes and are using them for game preserves.

"But they have to be fed—so we fed them with the discards of our nation. When these are not sufficient we throw down thousands of Middle-Men. I believe they prefer the bodies of Middle-Men to our discards. Perhaps the blood and taste are different.

"But just as soon as a growing unit—I believe you would call it a baby—is discarded, it is put into an inclined tunnel and shot down into a pit. Thus nothing, not even our immaturities, is wasted. Now if you will watch carefully, you will notice that my assistant is examining the first of a hundred incubators with units in them that are sufficiently aged to be started in nursery life.

"Perhaps of that hundred he will discard twenty-five. The specimens that are passed are taken to the nursery for an intelligence test. We consider that they are now a day old. At once they are taught by radio-hypnosis. The units are gone over once a year and all who do not make satisfactory progress are discarded.

"At the age of twenty their general education is at an end and they are divided into two hundred groups, each of which is given an intensive education in one specialty. From these groups, as necessity arises the new specialists are selected.

WE SELECT our Directors from a specially fed and prepared group. They have little responsibility but are excellent routine supervisors of our machinery. Practically all the finer work of our nation is done by specialized machines—I believe you call them robots. All that the directors do is to supervise these robots.

"Of course there is a lot of work that is so hard and dirty that we do not care to construct delicate machines to perform it and here we use the Middle-Men we have taken as slaves. We have perfected special machines to act as overseers and we have but little trouble in training the slaves to perform routine tasks.

"We have no time limit for the life of the directors. They simply go on working until they become inefficient and then we replace them.

"Rarely the Directing Intelligence determines that it would be best that his office be filled by a younger unit, chosen by a competitive examination. No one need take it who does not wish to. Only the three coordinators and the two hundred specialists are eligible. On the appointed day the candidates face the Directing Intelligence and are asked a number of questions.   The   candidate   who   passes   the   test   most successfully   is   chosen   as   the   rival   of   the   Directing Intelligence.

"With the three coordinators as judges, the two are tested and if the candidate worsts the Directing Intelligence the latter places himself in the Lethal Chamber and the new director takes office. The new head of our nation is at once cared for by the specialists in diet and internal secretion and as soon as he becomes a functioning male he spends half a year in the queens' house. He returns there once every twenty-five days.

"This was the method originated many thousands of years ago. For the last three thousands of years it has been slightly modified. The displaced ruler lives long enough, one or two hundred years, to impart his special knowledge to his successor. He is not required to do this but he may if he wishes to. The last four have kept on living.

"By this scientific method of renewing the units of our nation we have been very successful in raising the standard of intelligence. We have found that life is a great deal more comfortable without the female sex. We have always felt that it was best to absolutely segregate the queens. Now I am very much interested in your opinion of this propagating method. How does it appeal to you?"

"It's almost perfect," was the Englishman's enthusiastic response. "Personally, I have never had anything to do with women—for early in life I realized the fact that the more man associates with women the more he is hindered in making a success in his specialty. Now you say that the quality of your unit has been deteriorating—"

"Yes," the dwarf replied. "Our charts show that for eight hundred years there has been a steady increase in the number of rejected on the first examination. And even those that are retained have not the same qualities of intelligence, originality and adaptability as our standard prescribes."

Suddenly the specialist ceased speaking and removed from the voluminous folds of his gown a little black box, which he opened and on which he pushed a button. Then he held it close to his mouth and spoke a few words into it.

"The Directing Intelligence wishes us to return to his room," he said to Sir Harry. The latter nodded and, together with Wright and Ormond, followed the specialist out of the room.

When they were in the presence of the Directing Intelligence he spoke to them. "Tomorrow I am going to take you on a trip to some of our more important caves. Most of them are natural caves, greatly enlarged by our machines. All of our caves are connected by tunnels, through which we travel by means of cars, driven by atomic energy, which we learned to harness and control.

"It is very important that you obtain a thorough idea of our plans. Now that you are to be a consultant in anthropology we want you to obtain our viewpoint of everything. Have you a clear account of our process of reproduction?"

"A very satisfactory one. Your biologist is a remarkably clever man."

"It is well that you met him. Had you come a month later you would have found him replaced by his pupil. That young man is learned but has some peculiar ideas of his own importance. He hopes to become someday the Directing Intelligence of our nation."

"My word! What an ambition for a youngster to have. How crude of him to think that he could qualify!"

"Of course he has a right to if he can qualify. But the truth is that it is difficult to get enough candidates. For the last few hundred years there has been a growing disinclination among our members to accept responsibility. It's unprecedented.

"I will send for you in the morning. The coordinators will go into conference with me. We must replace our sociologist. He has been found wandering about our halls in a dazed fashion and insisted later on being permitted to enter the Lethal Chamber. He left no pupil and our decision will be a delicate one."

Once again the three Earthmen went back in their room. Ormond, as usual was silent. The Englishman looked a him out of one corner of his right eye. Wright walked over to the control table of the television screen and picked out the letters to form:

THE QUEENS' CAVE

He then pressed the red button. Immediately a picture of the room glowed increasingly distinct on the screen, until at last the women near the front went almost life-size. Wright looked at them carefully. Then he pressed the blue button. Not a sound was heard.

"These are peculiar women," commented the New Yorker. "Most peculiar. A room full of females and not one of them talking. But there is one thing about these women, Sir Harry. They do not seem to be well. Something is wrong with them."

CHAPTER TWELVE
More Captives

THE Englishman joined the New Yorker in his inspection of the picture. "The only thing I can see is that they all have large necks."

"That's it—goitre, *hyperthyroidism* and *exopthalmos.* Bet they are in a limestone country. Singular their medical specialist did not see that. What's this? There come two women. *Quick!* Press the blue button."

And as two clean fresh-looking young girls appeared on the screen voices came distinctly. "I don't care so much for myself, Joan—but I'm worried about you."

"That's all right, old dear. Not your fault. Although you insisted on going on the walking trip into this forbidden land I insisted on going with you—and then Aunt Charlotte insisted on going with us as chaperone and that's all there is to it. We were all determined to have our own way, so here we are. It's not your fault that we were captured by these monsters and put in the chamber of horrors. But what do you think happened to Auntie?"

"That is what makes me sick, Antoinette. That little dwarf told us very distinctly that we were to be sent to the Queens' house for an experiment—but he did not say a word about the old lady. Can you imagine her drawing herself up and saying in her regal tones, 'I am Miss Charlotte Carter of Cartersville, Carter County, Virginia. I demand that you release me at once, also my two charges, or I shall report the matter at once to my senators at Washington. D.C.?' "

"That was a long trip in that tunnel car, Joan. How far do you think we came and where do you think we are?"

"How can I tell? If this is the queens' house, I suppose these are the queens. Poor dears, how unhappy they look and how odd in every way…"

Wright pulled the lever with the yellow handle. Then he picked out on the keyboard:

MISS CHARLOTTE CARTER

He pressed the red button. In no time appeared a picture of a small cave with bars in front of it. Behind the bars was a fine-looking white-haired woman in a walking suit. Wright pressed the blue button and the woman spoke.

"Just wait until the President hears of this and there will be a most distinctly unpleasant time for these scoundrels."

"My word, Wright. She's fuming!" said Sir Harry.

"They're a hot-headed lot. Comes from one of those old Virginia families that knew Washington when he had to work for a living. A real aristocrat. Proud old lady, isn't she?"

"It seems so. One of the young ladies is her niece and the other a friend. Too bad they had to come across the border. My word. Too bad—but now they are here they will have to take the consequences. Right?" He winked slowly at Wright.

The New Yorker winked back and said, "Let them suffer. Probably flappers, seeking new sensations. They may find them in that cave. Gee…I sure am tired. Let's go to bed. Come on, Ormond, get some sleep. No use brooding because you'll never see any elephants down here. I'll show you something worth shooting tomorrow."

The next morning the spokesman of the three coordinators came to their room soon after they had finished breakfast. "The Directing Intelligence is ready for the journey," he announced. "Come with me. We are going to our large cave under the desert of Gobi at once."

In fifteen minutes they were seated in a small cigar-shaped car. The seats were double. In one pair sat the Directing Intelligence and Sir Harry. Behind them sat the coordinator and in the rear were the nonentities, Wright and Ormond.

"This is one of our earth-circling cars," explained the coordinator. "You will note the directing mechanism in the front of the car. It is simply another keyboard. We spell the name of our destination and the car goes to that place, being guided by a radio beam. All I have to do is to pick out the letters GOBI, press this lever and we are off."

The tunnel car shot forward at what seemed to be a moderate speed. The explorers were astonished when the coordinator whispered to Brunton that they were going at the rate of five hundred miles an hour and would even approach double that speed during the journey.

"NO DOUBT you are interested in the source of power, not only for the tunnel cars but for all our machinery. First, how do Middle-Men obtain power? Usually they convert the energy of coal into electrical energy by combustion. They use only an infinitesimal portion of the energy the coal contains. But we are able to take that same ton of coal and annihilate it and obtain eighteen billion times as much power from the ton of coal. If you knew the secret you could send one of your ocean liners from Europe to America and back again with the expenditure of a piece of coal smaller than a pea. We do that.

"With such a source of power the matter of speed is purely one of overcoming friction. That is a problem which we have not worked out up to the present time. Of course, we can go fast, probably more than a thousand miles an hour, though we find that such a speed is rarely advisable."

"Even at that rate it will take us some time to arrive at the Gobi cave," he continued. "At first you will think the cave is disappointing, because, on casual examination it is so similar to the cave at Reelfoot. But it is really very remarkable. In the first place it is a natural crater over five miles in diameter.

"Thousands of years ago our nation began digging into its walls and now we have an underground city that could, if emergency arose, accommodate the entire nation for a long period. The queens are kept in this cave and we also raise the young units there until they are past the nursery stage of life.

"You will be interested in our art gallery. For the last fifty thousand years we have been painting a history of our race on the walls of the Gobi cave. Every hundred years our artists do a mural that is characteristic of the most remarkable feature of that century.

"We do not care for the emotional side of art, but rather for its historical and social values. For that reason we have slowly accumulated the paintings and sculpture also of your races. Of course most of them are crude but at the same time they are worth preserving as a matter of record."

"It must be a remarkable collection," exclaimed the anthropologist.

"It is. So many things would have been destroyed by your Middle-Men had it not been for us. That library at Alexandria would have been completely burned by the Mohammedans but we were able to arrive in time to save over half of it. When Constantinople was captured we saved some of the best things in the city.

"And then we were careful, when we destroyed Atlantis, to save a great many of the art treasures of that country."

"My word! You must pardon me," interjected the Englishman, "but did I hear you right? Did you say you destroyed Atlantis?"

"Yes. It was a remarkable nation. But they were beginning to know too much. They were making such rapid advances in every branch of learning that they had to be destroyed. We felt that if they continued at that rapid rate they were apt to surpass us some day. We frequently destroy civilizations that annoy us. Sometimes we do this through our agents who obtain control of the countries by means of their superior intelligence."

AT THIS point the Directing Intelligence slowly turned his body and head until he was able to look at Brunton.

Then he joined the conversation.

"We have given considerable thought to the civilizations of the present day. If it were necessary we could produce a war more terrible that that of nineteen fourteen. Of course, it is a tedious cumbersome method. Our bacteriologist is working on this problem now and it may be that in a short time we shall be able, when we wish, to introduce diseases that will complete the destruction of the Middle-Men in a short time. He is a very brilliant worker and since he has started in experimentation on animals he has made some unusually rapid progress toward discovering the nature of life."

"So you believe in vivisection?"

"Absolutely. It is the only scientific method. We have used many of our captives for experiments in breeding. Many of the women killed themselves but we are more careful now. Would you like to see these laboratories?"

"I would indeed, sir. It would be a pleasure. The more I see of your nation the greater my admiration for your efficiency and your whole-hearted determination to allow nothing to interfere with your progress. You have never known the meaning of the words failure or discouragement."

"I am not so sure of that," was the peculiar reply.

For hours they shot through the tube—but at last the car came to a stop. The doors were opened and they walked out into a well-lighted hall and from there to a larger room, where a gathering of specialists and their pupils was awaiting them.

CHAPTER THIRTEEN
Charlotte Carter of Cartersville

FORMAL greetings were exchanged and then the entire party seated themselves at a long table. Food in abundance was placed before them. The food looked good, and had a fragrant odor that was more suggestive of flowers than vegetables.

As they ate, they tried to identify the various dishes—but finally even the Englishman had to admit that all were absolutely new to him. Some days later they learned the reason for their gastronomic ignorance. All of the foods were synthetic, prepared in the laboratory. The flavor, different in every dish, was placed there to enable the dwarfs to eat more heartily of the food. While bereft of emotion, they still retained their senses of taste and smell.

The three Earthmen, during the time they ate their synthetic food, had to acknowledge that though they had sufficient nourishment for all physical needs, they were never really satisfied. They were fifty thousand years behind the dwarfs, so far as their gastro-intestinal tracts were concerned. No matter how much they ate of the highly concentrated food they still longed for the meat and vegetables of their former life.

In a short time the table was cleared and the coordinator began, "The chief reason for this meeting is to introduce Harry Brunton to many of our specialists and induct him into his duties and privileges as consultant to the specialist in anthropology. He will have all the rights of the rest of the group and have authority to carry on experiments and researches covered by his specialty. We will now ask him to remove his clothes entirely so that we can clothe him in the robes of his profession."

Brunton had traveled all over the earth. He had been made a member and blood brother of more than one savage tribe. He passed through the uncovering of his body in public with a peculiar dignity that won the respect of all present. Shame was an emotion unknown to the underground race. But they knew that such an emotion existed among the earth people and they watched eagerly for its appearance in this noted stranger who had been selected by their Directing Intelligence to be one of them until his death.

A young dwarf now came forward with a white robe and assisted Brunton to drape it around his body, drawing the sash and tying it in a peculiar knot. Now the Directing Intelligence stood up and gave his charge in low emotionless tones.

"You, Harry Brunton, are now consultant to the Specialist in Anthropology for the people of Glow-wahr. In this position you will be given rights and powers inferior only to that of a specialist. You will at once select a pupil and bestow on him the wisdom that you possess in your special branch of intelligence. This pupil will be your guide.

"You are free to come and go as you wish throughout our realm. No door can be locked against you. But remember that for a long period you will be under the closest observation. The meeting is at an end. All will leave except the new consultant."

The coordinator walked up to Wright and Ormond and commanded them to go with him. "You need have no fear. Your master's position protects you. But you cannot stay here. Our ruler wishes privacy."

"Come and sit near me," said the Directing Intelligence to Brunton. "I want to talk to you about some private matters. I want to make life here as pleasant as I can for you, so that you may work more efficiently. Were there more like you on the Earth, we might be able to establish a reconciliation with your race.

"After talking over your future with the coordinators, I decided inasmuch as you are not yet unsexed, you would desire a female to live with. So we decided to secure a Middle-Woman for you—one of your own age and interested in anthropology and archaeology. She was a professor in these subjects at an American college for women and was one of a party of three women we picked up walking through Kentucky.

"Our specialist in machinery will make you a robot servant that can tame her until she is willing to submit to your authority. Her name is Miss Charlotte Carter. She will now be brought in."

In a few minutes the lady from Cartersville, Carter County, Virginia, walked in. She lost no time in making her demands. "If you men are the rulers of this savage country you will at once order my release and also that of the two young ladies of whom I am in charge—Miss Joan Summers and my niece, Miss Antoinette Carter. Our abduction was a most shameful affair and will call for the most severe reprisals as soon as Washington is notified of it."

The Directing Intelligence turned to the Englishman eagerly. "You will have to explain matters to her. She is your female and you will have to handle her."

"My word! Awkward position, Madam."

"I am not a madam. I am a Miss."

"My error. Pardon. You make me feel like wilted lettuce. But to business at once. This gentleman is the Directing Intelligence of a race of super-beings who are called the Ruling Minds of Glow-wahr. On the surface of Earth they are known as the 'Conquerors'—you may have heard of them.

"I am Harry Brunton and I have been given the honor of being made consultant to their specialist in anthropology. I will probably remain here the rest of my life. Without consulting me they decided to provide me with a female and for that distinctive purpose you have been brought here from America to this Gobi cave in Asia.

"You are here and you cannot return—so you had better make the best of it. Lots of things could happen to you down here worse than living with me. We are both interested in anthropology. Thus we shall have a great deal in common. I think that you had better be *nice* about it. My friends down here are not very familiar with ladies of the Earth and they might not treat you very well."

The Virginian lady walked up to the Englishman. "If you were the last man on Earth I wouldn't marry you!" she cried.

"My word! No one said anything about marriage," exclaimed Brunton. He turned to the Directing Intelligence.

"She cannot think. Reasoning is impossible for her. Marriage! My word! And I have refused a dozen of the prettiest heiresses in Europe! I'll tame her or shoot her down to the bone-makers. Have her taken out and washed and a white robe put on her and we will take her back to my apartment at Reelfoot."

"If you prefer we will send her to the Experimental Laboratory," said the ruler. "We thought you would want one of your own age. We will get you any kind of a woman you want."

"This one will do. But get her out at once."

As though in anticipation of his desires, two dwarfs came into the room, took the woman by the arms and led her out. The Directing Intelligence raised his hands and supported his head on either side with them.

"I have a peculiar feeling in my head. Five hundred years ago I could have faced any problem without difficulty. I could go for days without sleep. Now it is different. Perhaps this is the end. You heard what happened to our sociologist. The biologist tells the coordinators that the queens are not well and that the new units are of a very poor quality. The time may be ripe for the selection of a new Directing Intelligence.

"Of course, this is confidential. Whenever we change leaders there is always a period of uncertainty and unrest.

Perhaps we have too many Middle-Men working for us. They are always hard to handle. Perhaps the machine overseers are too severe. That happened once before and most of our Middle-Men were killed before we changed the machines to a less powerful voltage. A great many of the workers' deaths are suicides.

"It is becoming more difficult to secure material for our diffuse labor. Naturally our machines do a great deal. But there are some types of work that we have never been able to build machinery for. I am also bothered about our slaves. I want to dispose of them in some way. I want you to give it some thought."

AS though in obedience to an unspoken request the coordinator returned to the room, bringing with him Wright and Ormond. They were told to sit down. The Directing Intelligence turned to the coordinator.

"I want you to talk to them, then take the three of them out and show them the Zoological Gardens."

"The ruler of our nation directs me to explain some parts of our work to you," the coordinator said. "Many thousands of years ago, when we realized how far we were above the Middle-Men of our age, we also saw how impossible it was for them to preserve their national entity under the conditions of hardship and constant war and famine that they were exposed to.

"We saw also that many of the animals of that period were doomed to extinction unless they were protected in some way. For these reasons we started, long ago, making a collection of animals and races of men that we saw were becoming extinct. We have a name for this in our language but you can call it by a name familiar to you—zoological garden.

"It was an easy thing to do. We simply prepared large pits, holes in the earth, somewhat similar to the one at Reelfoot Lake. In each pit we placed a distinct form of life and tried to make the pit as close to its natural conditions of life as we could.

"For example the mammoth herd is placed in a pit high up in the Himalayas, where it is just cold enough for them to be comfortable and at the same time where there is a warm area to grow their food. We watch the herd carefully and remove all superfluous males. Thus we still have twenty mammoths, exactly the number that we started with.

"All of the reptiles and animals and birds represent species that are at present extinct on the Earth's surface. Some have only recently become so. Among the animals we class the original native of Tasmania. Of course he is a variety of Homo but never able to advance much above the lower Paleolithic culture. He was not a Neanderthal man, only a little better.

"When the Dutch discovered this island there were about five thousand of this race. In eighteen thirty-one there were only two hundred and three. Then we took a hand. Over thirty of the youngest and strongest were removed by us from Flinder's Island. The English thought that the inhabitants were dying fast but that was simply the result of our taking the best breeders.

"In eighteen seventy-six the last Tasmanian died and the race was believed by you to have been exterminated. In reality there are fifty-seven left in our zoological gardens, where we have imitated fairly well their original surroundings.

"We have done this with other peoples. The Australian aborigines are doing fairly well. They are uninteresting to study but were being killed off so rapidly that we considered it worthwhile to give them a home in our gardens. You can see these people someday. In fact, your special province will be their study.

"But these are simply sidelines of our most interesting work. Fully thirty-five thousand years ago we saw the necessity of preserving races that were bound to become extinct. In an isolated portion of Greenland we made a home for the Cro-Magnards. They are doing very well there and seem to be slowly developing mentally. They are fond of reindeer meat and have had no difficulty in adjusting themselves to the climatic conditions.

"With them, we have been able to keep alive the ibex, primitive horse, cave bear, and bison. You Middle-Men feel that you know something of the reindeer men from your study of the caves at Altamira, Aurignac and La Magdaleine. What would you think of being actually able to study the living people of the Aurignacian or Solutrean Ages?

"In Switzerland, surrounded by almost inaccessible mountains, we placed a colony of Lake Dwellers. They were fine examples of Neolithic culture but were bound to be destroyed by higher types. We took an entire colony from one of the Swiss lakes twelve thousand years ago and placed it where it could not be destroyed. They are doing very well, indeed.

"Without going into too great detail, that is the plan that we have followed all these centuries. When for any reason we saw fit to destroy a race we preserved a fragment of it, perhaps fifty persons, just enough to enable them to continue their existence. We made it possible for them to go on living the lives that they had become accustomed to. In not a single instance have we interfered with their culture.

"So, you will find in different parts of the world, many of them right here in our Gobi cave system, relics of the dim past, isolated from each other and from the world at large, living in our zoological gardens, our anthropological living museum.

"We will show you a colony of Tyrians—another little group of Carthaginians. Two thousand years before Christ, in your reckoning, we took fifty representative citizens from the city of Knossos on the island of Crete. They are living now as they did then. We even have a colony of Romans, haughty creatures, who are waiting for another message from their Mother City.

"When Alexander the Great took his Macedonians into Asia, we were able to isolate fifty of his soldiers in a crater in Afghanistan. We took Grecian women to them, and they are now one hundred and seventy in number. That is the way we have cared for these ancient peoples.

"There are perhaps seventy colonies in all and it will be your province to visit them and study them and care for them. We do not want them neglected in any way. We feel a definite responsibility in regard to them. I do not say that we admire any of them. Their culture is so far below ours that we feel they are almost another race.

"However, we are much interested in the modern citizen of the United States—I refer now to the city dweller. The Directing Intelligence feels that in his mode of life and surroundings he is unique. He asked one of the specialists to make a study of his habits, and the architect has been doing some work in the study and reproduction of his buildings.

"We have now ready an apartment house that will hold fifty couples. It is really a very remarkable duplication of a modern one-room apartment building in New York City. We have placed it in a new hole three miles in diameter. Suppose we take an air-machine and visit it?"

WITHOUT further invitation he walked out of the room, followed by Brunton and the two New Yorkers. After a short walk they came out on a landing where the flyer awaited them. The only resemblance that it bore to the airplane of the Middle-Men of 1930 was the fact that both traveled in the air. Then followed an exciting flight over the Gobi Desert and finally a gradual descent into a large hole.

"I think that we had better get into an automobile at once. We have a garage here, well supplied with Speedwells. It seemed that nothing less than a seventy-mile-an-hour car would satisfy. I suppose you Middle-Men can drive?"

"I can drive anything," boasted Ormond.

"Very well—get into a car and drive us around this circular track. Drive slowly, for I want to explain matters to you as we go. You see that here we are in the center of what might be called a miniature New York.

"We have a miniature moving-picture theater, a department store for the women to shop in, a delicatessen store and a self-service cafeteria for those who wish to dine out. There is no use of going into the apartment house. It is similar to thousands you saw every day in New York.

"On the other side of this hole is a small office building. You see, we have everything provided for. The women spend the day shopping while the men are at the office. At night they meet and either get their supper at the cafeteria or take it with them in paper bags from the delicatessen store to eat in their apartments. After supper they go driving or visit the movies.

"We made a special study of signboards and I am sure that you will be pleased with them. Look at that one!

CHEW CHERRY GUM
KEEP
JERKING JAWS JAZZING

"Every half mile we have a filling station and at frequent intervals a hotdog stand. Here and there we have planted violets, dogwood and wild azalea. We expect these to be rapidly torn up by the motorists and replaced by empty tin cans, waste paper and trash of all kinds but we will replace the wildflowers every year.

"The question of noise bothered us. We felt that fifty men and women could hardly be expected to make a satisfactory amount, even though each apartment has a radio and an automobile. So, we have placed a hundred noise machines in different parts of the hole. One button turns them all on. And when they are all on you New Yorkers are going to feel at home.

"Among other things will be this interesting feature—a part of the street will always be torn up. We felt that a finished New York would not be home at all. Also, right across the street from the apartment house is another apartment house. This will always be in the act of being torn down or built. You will always live within the sound of a steel riveter.

"We do not intend to make any change in your social life. That is for you to arrange. We are going to start with fifty men of a high type and their wives in the apartment house— and probably a hundred of the servant class in a tenement house at the other end of the street. You can divorce yourselves and remarry as often as you wish. There is only one stipulation and that is that you must keep up the number of the colony by an appropriate number of childbirths.

"And now I am going to ask the consultant in anthropology what he thinks of such a colony for the purpose of preserving the culture and refinement of the highest type of American citizenship?"

"I have no words to express my approval," replied Brunton. "I stayed for over two weeks in New York, and I feel that you have left little undone for the comfort of the average member of that community."

"It is well that it meets with your approval, for it concerns you rather deeply. We do not want your servants, Wright and Ormond, to be at large. They are not worthy of adoption into our race as we have done with you. We hate to place them with our degenerate workers and we were really at a loss as to their disposal. The thought came to us that we could place them in this colony."

CHAPTER FOURTEEN
Introductions

EVEN as he spoke another air machine came down from the skies and landed near them. The door of the cabin opened and out stepped two women. The pilot remained inside.

"Come over here," commanded the coordinator. "Gentlemen, I want you to meet Miss Joan Summers and Miss Antoinette Carter. Both are of the blond type which we find is popular at present. They are both accustomed to New York life, having spent the last seven winters there.

"Ladies, I want to introduce you to Sir Harry Brunton, late of England but now of our nation. He will do all that he can to see that your stay here is a pleasant one. The other two gentlemen are from New York and are both single. This is Mallory Wright, this is John Ormond."

The two girls stared at the coordinator but at last acknowledged the introduction. "Can you tell us the purpose of all this, Sir Harry, and just what has happened to our aunt?" asked Miss Summers.

"My word, yes! Awkward to tell you but your aunt is going to live with me. Wife, no doubt. You ladies are to marry these two New Yorkers and live right here with forty-eight other couples. I don't know which will marry which but you will have lots of time to decide that. If you find you have made a mistake you can change later on."

Miss Summers looked puzzled. "I never heard of such a thing! These men look like nice chaps but we don't want to marry them and I am sure that my aunt does not want to marry you or anyone else. Did she say that she would? Have you seen her?"

"I certainly have. She told me that if I was the last man on Earth she would not marry me—but I think she will have to change her mind."

"What did you tell her?"

"I told her that she will be fortunate to have a chance to marry me but that she is going to stay with me anyway. She was very much upset over it but she will cool down when she thinks it over."

"I wonder what the United States government will think about this?" asked Miss Antoinette Carter.

"That is immaterial," the coordinator replied. "In a few years there will be no United States, therefore, no government. Consultant, what do you want to do with these four persons?"

"I think they had better go back with us to the Reelfoot Lake cave. I am going to take their aunt there and the six of us can live together and get acquainted with each other. You are not ready as yet to open this New York colony. There are some finishing touches to do and the servants to be secured. Ladies, you will come with me? Your aunt will be with us."

"We are not going to go with you!" cried Miss Carter.

"I think you will! Coordinator, I understand that the human experimental laboratories are in this Gobi cave. Take us there. I want these young ladies to see what happens to other women not as fortunate as they."

"Wait a minute!" demanded Miss Summers. "What do you mean?"

"Simply this. These people are always experimenting with disease and germs. They perform these experiments on human beings, men and women like us. They keep them in wire cages like so many white rats and they do as they wish to with them, as we do with rats and monkeys. When they are done they open their bodies and study them and then throw them away. That is what might have been our lot.

"They take women and breed them for experimental purposes—and the odds and ends they use as mere slaves to do the hard work that they do not wish their sensitive delicate machinery to do. When they are worn out they feed them to wild animals. That might have been your lot.

"Instead, you are given the opportunity to marry two very nice fellows and live in a new apartment house with servants, automobiles, stores and restaurants at your command. Why not look at this matter in a sensible way! Your aunt and I will come and weekend with you."

"But it is all so new," whimpered Miss Carter.

"Life is that way. My word! I never thought that I would be a trusted unit in this nation of Conquerors. I have learned more new things in the last week than I ever would in the whole rest of my life. This colony will not be ready for occupancy for some time and until then you are to be my guests. Wright, can't you say something? My word! I thought you New Yorkers were fast workers."

"It is all very embarrassing," murmured the New Yorker.

"What does he mean by that word?" asked the coordinator.

"It is an emotion. I thought that no real New Yorker was ever embarrassed but it seems that I am wrong. Suppose we go back to the Directing Intelligence? Or is he through with us?"

"He wants to see you for a moment, Consultant, and then he thinks you had all better go back to Reelfoot."

"Then let us all get into the airplane. I think we shall be able to go in the same plane. It will be more *en famille.*"

ONCE again Sir Harry was alone with the Directing Intelligence. "I am not going back to Reelfoot with you," the ruler said. "I have been informed of your activities since you left me to look over our new colony, the miniature New York, and I think that you are wise to take the three women back with you for a little while until the colony is ready for occupancy.

"You have seen our colonies in what we call a living anthropological museum. I want to say that we have done our best to make these colonies self-supporting and perpetuating. Unless something happens which we have not been able to foresee, the Norsemen, the Tasmanians, the Carthaginians will still be in existence ten thousand years from now. Each preserves a splendid isolation from all the others. They live in little worlds of their own between which communication is impossible.

"The inventive mind of the present human race will spoil all this if allowed to follow its present trend. The average scientist of today among the Middle-Men is fond of prying into the waste places of the earth. Only by constant attention to details have we been able so far to prevent him from discovering our colonies, or, for that matter, ourselves.

"I am afraid that as a nation we are becoming decadent. We have not enough aim and ambition left to give us stimulating mental exercise. Perhaps as a race we are reaching our senility. I have entertained doubts at times as to the wisdom of our system of reproduction.

"For some time we have been annoyed by the Middle-Men. They have constantly interfered with our work. What is our work at present? Just this—we have done all we can on this planet. We wish to leave it and explore other worlds.

"We will come back to the Earth as a base—but we will add to our activities by conquering space and whatever forms of life we find there. At present we are making machines for interplanetary travel. That was one reason why we wanted the undisturbed possession of a part of the United States.

"When our plans are completed and our machines perfected we will close our caves here on Earth. We will make sure our robots are protected from rust; kill all the earth-slaves that we have in our caves; make final provisions for the comfort of our colonies and zoological gardens, and then send onto the Earth a plague that will, in a month, wipe out the human race, except those men and women who are kept as specimens. Only by doing this can we preserve the secret of our colonies.

"I think that it is a good plan to destroy the Middle-Men. They have not measured up to what we expected of them. Two hundred years ago we took selected specimens and sent them ideas and since then they have gone rapidly into a mechanical and electric age. But they have not made much use of their advantages. We feel that the time has come to destroy them.

"Following our custom we will, in as complete a manner as possible, preserve their so-called culture in our latest colony—one hundred men and women of the higher class and an adequate number of servants. At the proper time we will scatter the death germs over the Earth from our air machines, enter our interplanetary machines and seek other intellectual diversions. You will come with us'?"

"My word! *Stupendous!* The more I see of your race, the more I admire your intellectual attainments. I am proud to be one of you. But there are still some things that I do not understand; your large hands when you do no work? Your language and your perfect ability to speak in our language? And your remarkable control of your units?"

"All proper questions, and showing that you are far ahead of the average Middle-Man. For long centuries we used our hands a great deal—for we learned that there was a direct connection between the movement of our hands and the development of the brain. Naturally there came a time when our robots were so efficient that it was no longer necessary to employ manual labor. So the muscles have grown flabby but the size of the hands has remained.

"Our speech is different. It is really thought, which as you know is not dependent upon sound. Thus we could communicate, if we wished, with three men in three different languages and be perfectly understood by each, using only one series of thoughts.

"As for our government it is the most perfect absolutism that has ever been developed on this planet. You Middle-Men have never seen anything like it. Each individual has his own sphere of action in which he is supreme. But for over eighty thousand years, perhaps more, no unit has dared to dispute any matter with the Directing Intelligence. I could order the entire nation to enter the Lethal Chambers and they would go at once without hesitation. Now is there anything else that I can explain to you?"

"YES. I am interested in these Middle-Men that you have here. Do they never revolt, attempt to destroy you in search of their freedom? What is their mental condition?"

"Revolt is not unknown to us. Ten thousand years ago we had to kill most of them and start over again. The replacements are very numerous. Some live for five years but many are good workers for only a few months. We thought that if we had as many women as men they might be more content but it made only more trouble. The women wore out too fast. The men killed each other, fighting over the women.

"A century ago we started a new plan. As soon as a Middle-Man or woman is brought down here he or she is operated on and made sexless. As neutrals they work better and last longer. Lately we have been experimenting with mental diseases and have inoculated all of the Middle-Men with the germs of dementia praecox. When this disease develops they make very good workers and become quite strong and fat."

"How many of them would be able to resume their surface life if they were returned?"

"Practically none. Even with those who have been well cared for in the cages of our experimental laboratory there would be an inability to readjust themselves to a surface life. For centuries we have been trying biological experiments to make a new race of workers. I suppose we have used five thousand women of different nationalities in these experiments. At present there are three hundred white females in our biological laboratories. Naturally, they would rather die than return to their families."

"My word! Yes. As usual you are right. They are all better off dead. I suppose that when you kill the rest you will also empty the cages in your laboratories?"

"Yes, they will all be emptied and thoroughly cleaned and sterilized, to make ready for any new specimens that we bring back from other worlds."

"Your whole idea is wonderful!" exclaimed Sir Harry. "When will you start your interplanetary trip?"

"The preparations are nearly completed. Our space machines are examples of mechanical perfection. Trial flights in them have shown the soundness of the engineering details. The same force will be used that is used to drive our tunnel cars, the complete annihilation of small pellets of coal. There is only one factor in our national life that is causing us concern. Until that detail is solved we cannot hope to make a success of our interplanetary conquests."

"As a member of the nation, vitally interested in its welfare, may I ask just what it is that disturbs you?"

"You may. For centuries there has been a constant increase in our intelligence and efficiency. We have probably attained the apex of possible mental growth. But, for over fifteen centuries, there has been a gradually increasing apathy, a disinclination to progress as individuals.

"When a coordinator or a Ruling Intelligence feels that the time has come for replacement it is almost impossible to find anyone willing to become a candidate for the position. The situation is especially trying in regard to the Directing Intelligence. As you know, he is the father of the race. There has come the thought that, due to constant intermarriage and an absence of new blood, perhaps the nation has become decadent.

"The study of the history of the various nations of Middle-Men shows that the average nation lives about fourteen hundred years. We felt that our nation, composed as it was of individuals who would never die were it not for the best interests of the country, might live on forever. But now enters this strange psychic apathy, this unwillingness to assume greater responsibilities. How can it be explained?"

"Pride is one of the emotions you have deprived yourselves of."

"I understand that. But this situation is not to be explained by the absence of the emotion of pride. Take the case of the specialist who was found wandering around our halls in a dazed condition, muttering over and over that he wanted to be led to the Lethal Chamber. There was a case of some form of acute mental disease, and I fear that this same condition exists in a chronic condition among most of our specialists.

"Our psychiatrists have studied a few of the worst examples and feel that, unless we can be confident of correcting this part of our mental life it would be best not to go ahead with our space explorations. Of course, we will follow out the program as far as the destruction of the Middle-Men is concerned."

Sir Harry rubbed the back of his head thoughtfully. "I have done a lot of exploring in Australia," he at last said, "and I met an isolated tribe of Bushmen there who presented some very interesting problems for study. I lived with them nearly a year, finally being able to understand their language well enough to follow their thought.

"They had been completely isolated from all other tribes for so many centuries that every child was the product of the most intensive inbreeding. The entire tribe was related to each other. Their decay was so fast that they have already died out. The remarkable part of their existence was the fact that they did not seem to care what happened. They were without emotion and without incentives.

"By Jove! It occurs to me that those Bushmen had something in common with your nation. There is certainly psychic resemblance. Perhaps I could, with Wright to help me, do something—but perhaps this is not the time to mention such a possibility."

"I suppose you mean that you could help us?"

"Something like that."

"Perhaps that is what made us bring you here?"

"That might be. But suppose you were able to make this trip into space, explore other worlds besides ours? You still feel that it would be necessary to destroy the Middle-Men?"

"I believe so. They seem so useless and so inefficient. And we may wish to return and take possession of the entire Earth."

The Englishman sighed. "If that is all that you want to talk about I must ask you to excuse me. This has been hard day for me, and I think it would be best to return to our apartments at Reelfoot Lake."

"You have my permission to depart. Think about that psychic apathy and see what can be done about it."

CHAPTER FIFTEEN
Hopelessness

THE new consultant was leaving the room when the Directing Intelligence called him back. "I wish you would give the matter of headaches a little thought. My cerebral pains are becoming almost disabling at times. I would long ago have allowed myself to be replaced had there been any candidates. I wish you could help me in some way."

The Englishman promised to do his best. The journey back to the Reelfoot Lake cave was a silent one.

Sir Harry Brunton looked old. In his white robe he seemed like a Roman senator, deliberating with sorrow on the debilities of the new generation. He leaned back in his seat, folded his arms and shut his eyes.

Miss Charlotte Carver was equally silent. In spite of her protests she had been bathed and almost disinfected. When it was finished she was forced to admit to herself that she had never been so clean in her entire life. After this she was clad in a single white robe which reached to her ankles. It was warm but even to her old-fashioned ideas absolutely without style. She knew she looked a fright. No wonder her nieces had almost snickered when they first saw her!

The two girls, however, had other things to think of. They had not only been captured, they were being threatened with life in an insane asylum, called a "New York miniature colony," as wives of two New Yorkers, who had also been captured. The whole arrangement seemed like a dream. The worst part of it was that the two men were evidently as opposed to the marriage as the women were. No courtesies had been exchanged since the introduction. The girls thought that the boys might at least be civil.

The two men were not to blame. Their past life in New York had been but a poor preparation for the adventures they had been through since they had left the metropolis. The most depressing part was a constantly growing despair. They realized that their captors were indeed "Conquerors." Whatever these strange people planned, they accomplished.

They felt doomed. They were not native born, but they had lived in New York long enough to love the city in spite of its defects. They felt that the model was a pitiless caricature of everything that was bad and useless in the metropolitan life. Surely all of New York was not like that. It was not fair.

Wright determined that he would show them. They had made a city for a hundred persons of the better classes and in a tenement house they were going to put a hundred or more servants. He was going to be mayor of that city and then he would show them! Those silly signs were going to come down and be used for firewood. The wild flowers would be cultivated and the whole pit made into a gorgeous natural park. There would be an end to the hot dog stands and the cooking would all be done in the homes.

Ormond sat moodily, his chin pressed down on his collar, and now and then swore softly to himself. Taking everything into consideration it was not a very merry party.

AT LAST they were back in the rooms Sir Harry Brunton had called his apartment. Miss Charlotte Carter had done a lot of hard thinking and had made up her mind to open the conversational game.

"I have a proposition to make to you, Mr. Brunton or Sir Harry or whatever you call yourself. These girls are my nieces, one by blood, the other by adoption. I am responsible for their being in this trouble.

"I want to make a bargain with you. I will stay here with you. That does not mean that I like you any more than I did yesterday. It does not mean anything. It simply means that we won't be fighting all the time. It does not make any odds to me whether you marry me or not.

"I think that, if I have to spend my life down here with these monstrosities and wear this kind of clothing, nothing that happens to me will make any difference. But I promise you that I will be as nice to you as I can if only you will let these poor girls go back to their parents and the sweet sunshiny Earth again. Will you?"

The young women rushed to her and started to kiss her.

"You sweet thing!" Miss Summers cried. "Do you think we would let you make that kind of a sacrifice for us? Not at all! I was just going to make the same proposition. We girls will stay with these two men and help them start their silly old colony if only they set you free. I suppose Sir Harry is a nice enough man. But at your age—"

"My dear child! Why do you say 'at my age'? Please remember that I am the youngest of my family and, in spite of the fact that my hair is white, I am only ten years older than you. No! If anyone makes the sacrifice it must be me. I think this man is going to be a gentleman even if he does look like a fool in that bathrobe."

At this Miss Antoinette Carter started to laugh and then cry. It was too much for Ormond. He had sisters at home. Awkwardly he put his hand on the girl's shoulder.

"Don't do that, Miss Carter, please don't. It is bad enough as it is for all of us without breaking down. We are going to do everything we can for you and the other ladies—though just what we can do is a question. Don't mind our friend and the way he talks. He has a very important position with the new government and, of course, he has to do what is expected of him."

When Mallory found how nicely his friend was taking care of an awkward situation and a beautiful girl he lost no time in trying to be equally courteous to Miss Joan Summers. Sir Harry looked on in silence. At last he started to grin.

"It seems to me, Miss Carter, that perhaps your proposed sacrifice for your nieces would not be appreciated."

And even the former professor of anthropology was forced to admit to herself that worse things might have happened to the girls than be made to marry these two men and live in a colony.

But the Englishman had some things to say to his companions. He lost no time in asking them to sit as close together as they could and listen to him. The girls were feeling much better by this time and had even found that they knew some people in New York whom the two younger men knew and had seen a good many of the same shows.

"My word! but this is an odd situation to be in," began Sir Harry, "and I am not sure that I shall be able to make myself understood. But here's trying. We are all here together in the same boat. We may think that we are in tough luck—but our situation is Paradise compared with the poor men and women who are down here as slaves.

"As you know, I am what you might call a Conqueror myself. I had nothing to do with Miss Charlotte Carter's being brought here and I was as much surprised as she was when I found out just why they did it. I have never married. I never found a lady who would look at me twice. So I have spent my time just wandering. I have money but I never had a real home. My parents died when I was young and after that I had neither kith nor kin.

"It looks as though I am going to stay here. If Miss Carter wants to stay with me as a fellow scientist I promise her that she will be treated with the greatest respect. In England I was known as a man and here I am the first Middle-Man to be given the rights of a Conqueror. I do not say this boastfully but I want Miss Carter to know that I have been considered a gentleman all my life. She will find me one.

"Now in regard to these young people. Their condition might be worse than it is. Unless something unexpected happens, the Middle-Men in the New York Colony will be the only members of our race alive. In that colony they will lead the lives of pampered pets. The Conquerors will do all that they can to make the life of that colony secure and successful. So far as I can see they have neglected nothing.

"I am going to keep you five people right here with me for a while. Things may happen in the future that seem odd but always remember that I have your interests at heart. I would like to do something for the slaves—but their doom is sealed. Now, how about a jolly six-handed game of poker—or would you rather play bridge while I tell your aunt about the colony of Tasmanians?"

THE next morning, immediately after breakfast, Sir Harry took Mallory Wright to one side.

"Listen, my lad. I brought you along to have the services of a true scientist if the need for one arose. Well, to make short work of a long subject, let me say that there is something for us to do. I think that you and I have it in our power to do something rather fine if only we can put it across. Did you ever do any biochemistry?"

"A little, working with serums and antitoxins."

"You are at home in a chemical laboratory?"

"Yes, I think so."

"Then we will get busy. There is no doubt that these people have the laboratory and everything in it that is necessary for our work. Suppose we tell Ormond to keep the ladies entertained? We will put in some hard work in experimentation. I shall have to leave most of the actual work to you but I will give you the ideas."

"What are we going to do?"

"First, study these Conquerors. It is no secret that they are sick. We must find out just what that disease is and the cause of it. Then we must find a cure. When we have that cure, then we can start in to play poker."

"Poker?"

"Yes, with our race as the stake. Your nation and mine—their future destiny. My word! What a game that will be..."

Wright's jaws tightened. "I'll do my best," he said tensely.

The Englishman slapped him on the back. "Good lad," he muttered. "I knew you would. True gold is your metal."

From that morning on the three ladies and Ormond saw little of their friends except at mealtimes—and even then they were not very satisfactory table companions. A complete laboratory had been constructed in one of the rooms in the apartment and there the two men, with various specialists to assist them, spent most of their time.

Sir Harry felt safe in having these Conquerors assist him. They had certain knowledge that was valuable to him but they seemed curiously unable to value or apply their knowledge. The specialist in organic chemistry realized that fact and commented on it to Wright one day.

"There is no doubt," he said, "that our knowledge is very complete. But for many years it has seemed to be almost useless. Our specialist in statistics told us at a recent annual meeting that our inventions are now only three one-hundredths as numerous per century as they were five thousand years ago.

"Of course we might say, as a defensive reply, that there is hardly anything left to invent. But that would not be true. We simply have reached a point at which we do not use the knowledge we have. Either we cannot use it or we lack the psychic urge to do so.

"Perhaps, if some great calamity overpowered us, it would act as a mental stimulus, but otherwise—oh, well—it seems that we do not care. And so we simply spend our days in rehearsing the knowledge we have and our nights in broken slumber, disturbed by headaches."

His story was but a variation of the confession made by the Directing Intelligence to Sir Harry. The leader of the nation had not exaggerated the difficulty. It was apparent to most of the specialists that something very serious was wrong with the psychic life of the nation.

Day by day Sir Harry and Mallory Wright worked on. They made an intensive study of the ichor, the fluid that flowed through the circulatory system of the Conquerors instead of the rich red blood of the normal human being. They studied this ichor from every possible point of attack. At times Wright became so tired of this mysterious ichor that he rebelled at any further study. But the Englishman urged him on.

"Hang onto it, Mallory, old top. Bite into it and clamp your jaws. Right there is the thing we are after, the hidden ace that is going to win our poker game for us. It is their blood—and blood means life. My word! I know that little girl is hungry for your companionship but you must work."

And Wright would wipe his worried brow and start to work again.

One day the specialist in bacteriology came sauntering into the laboratory. His face was as emotionless as the faces of all the race but in his eyes there was a peculiar glitter.

"I have felt better for a whole week," he told Sir Harry. "For months I have done but little work. A few days ago I started and now I am through. I have discovered and perfected a strain of microbes, deadly bacilli, that will so quickly destroy the Middle-Men that they will all be dead before they realize what is wrong with them.

"The rest will be easy. All we have to do is to make a large amount and scatter it over the earth from our airplanes. The making of a preventive to give to the human beings in our various colonies will be easy. Of course we do not want them to die with the other Middle-Men."

"I guess the human race is better off dead," commented Sir Harry. "It seems that they have not merited the right to survive."

"No, they are doomed," replied the specialist as he sauntered out of the laboratory.

"From now on," whispered the Englishman to Wright, "we work alone—and when I say work I mean it!"

CHAPTER SIXTEEN
Anxious Days

BUT it seemed that their very need, their overwhelming desire to accomplish their purpose, thwarted them. Again and again they seemed on the verge of success only to be again faced by failure. It remained for Miss Charlotte Carter to break through the hard surface of the scientific enigma and give them a starting point toward success.

"Something has to be done," she announced emphatically. "Time is passing and whatever dangers we face are growing more and more threatening. You two men have become absolutely antisocial. You act as though no one existed except yourselves. I think that we ought to talk the problems over and see if we cannot help you. You have spent so much time in worried thinking that there is just a possibility of your brains becoming dull."

The Englishman finally agreed. He realized that such a procedure had its dangerous elements. Suppose they were being carefully watched all the time by the television machine? It might end in the death of all of them. At the same time, he knew that there was a great deal of truth in what the lady from Virginia said. So he yielded.

There was another conference. Ormond, as usual, was polishing his big rifle. The two young women sat next to each other. They were more interested in the development of the New York Colony than in the experimental work that was being performed in test tubes. Mallory Wright sat for the greater part of the discussion with his face buried in his arms on the table. He was tired and mentally exhausted. Even Sir Harry talked with the greatest effort in order to put the problem in such shape that Miss Charlotte Carter would understand.

"My dear sir. How simple! You have been trying to make a compound which, injected into the circulation of these dwarfs, will restore their mental poise, give them inspiration to do their work and solve their problems. You have been working at it from the standpoint of their internal secretions. Terrible!

"They lack something and you have it. I suppose you know by this time the exact composition of their blood. Make a similar examination of ours and determine the difference. See what there is that you have which they lack.

Put those missing elements into a compound and inject it into them."

"But—my word! Miss Carter! Clever and all that—but there are twenty thousand of them. It would exsanguinate me to furnish them all with my blood."

"I never thought that you would. I simply said that you should find the difference and make a compound out of your blood—just enough for an analytical study. Then make a formula of that compound and produce it synthetically in the laboratory. Memorize the formula and never, never put it down on paper. Try it, Harry. Oh, I wish that you would let me help you!"

After that work started anew. The three, for now Miss Carter spent her days in the laboratory, began to work with new vigor. She had given them a possible solution of the puzzle and with that new thought to work on their progress was rapid. In a week, they had the compound formed out of Sir Harry's blood. In three more days they knew its exact composition and in another week they had made about a gallon—enough to cure over a hundred of the dwarfs or their psychic apathy.

The last few days Sir Harry insisted on doing all the work himself. He explained to his companions that something might happen to Wright and it would be necessary for the work to go on.

THEY had been able to manufacture a synthetic serum which they believed would solve the secret of the decadence of this strange race. Ormond, in one of his few periods of loquacity, made no effort to hide his idea of the folly of such a step.

"Give them time," he explained to Miss Antoinette, "and they will find that we have double-crossed them. If I had been Sir Harry I would have bluffed them, delayed the laboratory work, done everything I could to put them off from month to month and never, never have deliberately produced a drug that would make them more efficient than they are already."

"What is this poker game he is always talking about, John?"

"That poker game is like my elephant gun. It is just a specimen of his humor. He told me to take my elephant gun—said that one could never tell what need there might be for it. Once a day since then he has asked me if the gun is in good condition. Have I shot it? I have not! That is the way with this poker game. Just an example of his English humor."

Perhaps Sir Harry knew how some of how his party felt—but if he did he showed no signs of it. He simply went on with his work. With Miss Charlotte beside him constantly he was brighter than before, smiled a little, even laughed at times. Then one day he filled a glass syringe with the new solution, carefully placed it and a sterilized needle in his pocket, said goodbye to his co-workers and went out.

The time had come to play poker.

Three hours later he was sitting at a table around which were grouped the Directing Intelligence and the three Co-ordinators.

Sir Harry lost no time in telling them the reason back of his asking for the conference.

"Some months ago the ruler of your nation took me into his confidence. He stated that our nation, for you know that I have been made a Conqueror by adoption, is threatened with a situation so serious that, until it can be solved, all thoughts of the exploration of space would have to be abandoned. He asked me to try to do something.

"First, let me take up the less serious conditions. Your queens have a condition known among my former race as hyperthyroidism. It is nothing more nor less than an enlargement and over-secretion of the thyroid gland in the neck. I am sure that the condition is the result of an excess of iodine in their food and water.

"Give them quinine hydrobromate to reduce their pulse rate, add extract of ergot if necessary, take the excess of iodine away from their food and water. I am content that their health will be so greatly improved that the future units of our race will be healthier in every way.

"The second minor problem is the one of your constant headaches. As I have reason to know from my past studies your brains are very large. Consequently, the blood vessels in your skulls are huge and I believe that the pressure of circulation is the main cause of the headaches. I will take that up with the specialist in medicine and suggest to him the proper treatment—though I am sure that just as soon as I give him the hint he will be able to go ahead. I am just surprised that he was not able to see what was the matter himself."

The Directing Intelligence slowly turned his head until his large dilated eyes were fastened on the Englishman. Then he spoke.

"There is no reason for your being surprised. He has had the same mental inertia that has overcome all of us. Our stagnation has become almost complete. For over a thousand years our space machines have waited, unoccupied, for the completion of our program.

"Some of our specialists have been seriously ill, others have just been mentally dull, not one of us has been normal—by that I mean the norm of our race ten thousand years ago. Our replacements have been many but not in the positions of trust and responsibility. I want to give you an example. I will send for the specialist in medicine and show you just why he was unable to solve these problems that seem to your active mind to be so easy."

After fifteen minutes of waiting the specialist in medicine walked into the room and took a chair at the table. "Have you any reports to make?" asked the Directing Intelligence.

"None."

"One hundred years ago I asked you to make a thorough study of the queens and see what was necessary to improve their health. Have you done that?"

"I have. But I am unable to solve the problem of their illness."

"Have you arrived at any idea as to the cause of my own headaches?"

"No. I have the same trouble myself. I try to work on these questions. I know all about medicine that was ever known by our nation. But for some reason I seem to be unable to use that knowledge efficiently."

The Directing Intelligence turned to Sir Harry. "This is a very good illustration of why the interplanetary journey has been postponed for hundreds of years."

"I understand. But suppose I have a drug that will restore his mental vitality, make him capable of using the vast store of knowledge he undoubtedly possesses? If I can do that with him will you believe that I am capable of doing the same to the entire race?"

"I will believe. If it can be done with one it can be done with all. But have you the drug?"

"I have. I brought one dose of it with me."

"You have my permission to give it to this specialist."

BRUNTON walked over to the physician and rolled up his sleeve. From one pocket he took out a rubber tube, which he applied above the elbow as a tourniquet. From another pocket he took out the sterilized needle and the syringe. Then he painted the skin in the fold of the elbow with a red antiseptic. Already the veins were beginning to be prominent.

"I have in this syringe," began Sir Harry, almost as though he were lecturing to a class of students, "twenty cubic centimeters of a serum which I intend to give through the vein. Thus it will enter the circulation at once and in a few minutes the nervous system, especially the brain. I believe that one dose will be sufficient to establish the potency of the drug.

"Of course, later on it may be necessary to repeat the treatment—but that is a matter of secondary importance. Now I will puncture the vein slowly and empty the syringe into it. The operation, as you see, is practically painless. There! It is all over. Now I hope in a couple of weeks we will see the results."

The next two weeks that passed were filled with the most terrible anxiety for the six Earth-beings. Attempts at gayety fell flat as all waited under growing tension for a call from the Directing Intelligence. It was understood that the specialist who had been treated was to remain in isolation during the period so that the effect of the medicine might be more properly evaluated.

At last the call came. A white-faced Sir Harry Brunton, barely able to maintain his jaunty air, found himself in the presence of the Directing Intelligence, his coordinators and the treated specialist. Throughout the room a deathlike silence reigned until the Directing Intelligence spoke to the specialist.

"How do you feel?"

"Somehow I feel better. My mind seems to be clearing. Now in regard to that problem of the health of the queens. There is no doubt that they are receiving too much iodine and that has caused an overproduction of thyroid juice. We will give them quinine hydrobromate, reduce the iodine content in their diet—and I feel sure that they will soon be well."

"How about the headaches?" asked the Directing Intelligence.

"I see the cause now. The blood pressure is too high. Nitrates will reduce the pressure and cure the headaches."

"I asked you the same question many years ago. You took a long time to answer."

"I realize that. But I could not think then. I can now. This new medicine has given me wonderful vitality, mental alertness, an ability to use my accumulated knowledge. In someway I feel that I have been sick but I am all right now. I feel as if I were a new man."

Sir Harry began to smile. "My word! It worked as expected!"

"It did," acknowledged the Directing Intelligence. "How soon can you start in treating the entire nation?"

The Englishman rose to his full height. He towered above the seated dwarfs.

"There are a few things that I want to make clear. In the first place I am the only living person who knows how to prepare this drug. I have enough to treat about one hundred persons. After that it will be necessary to make more and I am the only one who can do it. I want you to understand that fact. I am the only one. Now I am anxious to make enough to cure the entire nation, because I want you to go on that interplanetary journey and I want to go with you. In fact I think that you need me."

"But life as I see it is largely a matter of compromises, gives and takes. Of course you have ruled so long that you can see no viewpoint except your own. I want to help you but I want to be paid. I want you to promise me that you will make no effort to kill the Middle-Men, the race I come from, until we return from the space trip. There will be time enough then to deal with them as you wish.

"The second request is for permission to liberate my five fellows and send them back to their comrades and their civilization. I am sure that they can be trusted to keep their adventures here a secret. In fact I will myself be a bond to make sure of that. If you will grant me these two requests I will start at once making enough of the drug to cure the entire nation of this peculiar devastating mental illness."

Though they were incapable of showing emotion by facial change there was a deadly glitter in the eyes of the dwarfs who looked up at him. The Directing Intelligence expressed their thought.

"Impossible! Why should we bargain? You are here and in our power. Suppose we force you to show us how to make the drug and then kill all of you?"

"You can do a part of that—but remember, I am the only one who knows every step of the process whereby this drug is made. If I do not make it, it will not be made. I anticipated your refusal, so I came prepared to play what we call poker with you.

"I hold in my hand a thin glass vial, containing a few drops of a deadly poison. I am going to place it between my teeth. If you refuse to agree with my suggestion I will crush the glass and die. Then, where will you be?"

He placed a large glass bead in his mouth and closed his lips.

HE SAT down and faced them. For five minutes there was a conflict of wills, a battle of intellects. Then the Directing Intelligence spoke. "We will grant your requests. After all, we need a person like you with us when we take the journey into space. You have something that even the best of us lack—perhaps it is youth.

"I will give orders that the Middle-Men be not harmed. The New York Colony will remain closed and your five companions will be liberated—on condition that you remain with us, make enough of the drug to cure the race and take the journey into space when our nation starts on its explorations of the unknown."

Sir Harry took the glass bead out of his mouth and put it in his pocket. "That's a bargain," he replied. "I am confident that it is the best thing to do for everybody."

"By the way," asked the Directing Intelligence. "You said that this was a poker game. What did you mean by that?"

The Englishman took out the little glass bead and rolled it on the table.

"My word! Had to explain. Poker is one of those American games. It is built on a bluff. You pretend at times to have cards when your hand is devilish poor. Take that glass bead, for example. It is solid. No poison in it. Well, I must go. I am going to be busy, making over nineteen thousand doses of that medicine. You can go on with the program now and have the definite assurance that everything will be all right."

He walked out of the room. The dwarfs looked at each other. One of the coordinators broke the silence.

"He is a very capable man. Knowing one thousandth of what we knew he was still able to make such good use of his little knowledge that he won the game of poker—as he so peculiarly expressed it. Well, our word is passed and after all we can kill those Middle-Men when we return from our voyage through space. For we know now that we are going and we know that we will return."

The Directing Intelligence added, "At least we know that a capable consultant is going with us."

CHAPTER SEVENTEEN
A National Treatment

THE Englishman returned to his five companions. Ormond was still polishing the elephant gun. The two young women were whispering to each other. Wright was trying to console the elder Miss Carter, who was crying.

"Cheerio!" cried Sir Harry. "What mean these tears at the point of victory? There is a tide in the affairs of men which taken at its flood leads on to fortune and we are all swept with that tide to a happy ending of our adventure. You are going home—do you understand? Back to the States and your little old New York. The game of poker was played and we won."

"Yes, Harry," said Miss Charlotte, amid her sobs. "We know all about the way you won. We had you under observation in the television machine from the time you left us until you started to come back. We know what you did to secure our freedom. It was nothing much, was it?

"Just a promise on your part that you would go with them to Mars or Saturn or Venus or wherever it is they are going. Just a promise that you would stay with them until you died of old age—and all to get liberty for us. What do you suppose that I—I mean, what do you suppose we care about New York if we know all the time that you are with these horrid monstrosities?"

"Now, Miss Charlotte," pleaded the Englishman, "please do not talk that way. I am sorry you used the television screen. My word! Your scolding me that way makes me feel like wilted lettuce. And all the time I was thinking that I had done something worth while in securing your liberty and saving the human race, at least for a little while."

"It was fine," chimed in Wright. "You were wonderful but Miss Charlotte naturally feels that all of us ought to have stuck together in this adventure."

"I do not want you to look at it that way. You should consider the welfare of our race, the men and women, the Middle-Men, who are trying to make a success out of life by attaining to happiness and are making such a botch of it. You go back to them. Go back as missionaries. Show them that there is something more in life than just fame and wealth. Try to develop a spirit of national sacrifice, a unified soul that will be able to face any threatening danger and triumph.

"Now let us go to the laboratory. Just as soon as we make enough serum and give it I am going to send you five dear people back home. You will help me, won't you, Miss Carter?"

"I'll help all I can, but nevertheless I despise you for the way you are acting."

"And I suppose," said Ormond, "that while you are working, I can go ahead and polish the elephant gun and take the ladies on sightseeing expeditions?"

"Don't forget the elephant gun," advised Sir Harry, laughing.

For the next week the three scientists worked long hours in the laboratory. Over nineteen thousand doses of the life-restoring drug were ready for use. Word was sent to the Directing Intelligence to assemble the nation at the Reelfoot Crater. Five days later every unit was present—the Directing Intelligence, the Coordinators, the specialists and the directors.

Often in the past they had assembled to witness the peculiar rites of their nation and watched long lines of discards pass silently and without emotion into the lethal chamber. Now, for the first time, they had gathered for a constructive purpose. Word had been sent that they were all to be given a dose of a new serum that would restore the intellectual vitality of the nation.

After that they would all go into space—greater achievements, to larger glories and conquests. They were emotionless but one and all they were doing a lot of thinking. Even the dullest among them realized that it was an occasion that promised much for the future of their nation. Sir Harry, Mallory Wright and Miss Charlotte stood near spotless tables, where they were assisted by a number of specialists who had received their treatments a few days before.

Then the line of dwarfs, headed by the Directing Intelligence and the coordinators, moved forward. Each unit, as he passed the table, was given an intravenous injection of the serum. Hour after hour they passed while, hundred by hundred, the nation was restored to vitality and mental vigor. Muscles ached, brains reeled, the limit of endurance was reached—still the three scientists kept on and at last, nearly dropping from fatigue, they reached the end of their labor. The entire nation of Conquerors had been treated.

SIR Harry told Wright to take Miss Charlotte back to the apartment. Then he walked, showing utter exhaustion, up to the chair where sat the Directing Intelligence.

"My part of the contract has been fulfilled," he whispered. "My word, but it was a greater task than I thought it would be. Tomorrow I want to send the five back to their homes and their friends. Will it be all right?"

"It will be all right. Bring them to the edge of the crater. The radio-controlled boat will be in readiness for them. Place them and their baggage in the boat and I will see that they are taken to Tiptonville. From there they will find their own way. They will not be harmed. You, Sir Harry, have won the undying gratitude of our nation. You shall be repaid by being permitted to go with us into space."

"That will be quite jolly."

"What do you mean?"

"Oh! That is an emotion. You could not understand but I shall be glad to go. Remember, you have promised not to destroy the Middle-Men until you return."

"I remember. Now I must start to prepare for the trip. I feel new life, new mental vigor. The entire nation will have new life. I suppose you will want to spend the rest of your time with your companions before they leave?

"Yes, I will go and say goodbye to them."

"You show no emotion at the thought of leaving them?"

"I am too tired to show anything."

"SO TOMORROW," Sir Harry concluded, "you five are going to get in the little boat and go back to Tiptonville. From there you can get to New York. Once there communicate with the British Consul and he will pay you. Wright, you go over to London as soon as you can, and see the Prime Minister and give him an outline of these weeks. I suppose the President of your country will be interested.

"Tell him that I consider that there is no immediate danger but they should consider the future years very carefully and see what they can do. I do not want any offensive taken against the people who have adopted me."

"And are you going to stay with them all the rest of your life?" asked Miss Charlotte Carter in a low tone.

"I think so. I gave them my word of honor to do so for as long as they need me and want me. That was one of the prices I paid for your liberty. You five can go back now to— your loved ones—"

"Oh! How clever you are—back to our loved ones!" She left the room, saying over her shoulder, "You must excuse me. I shall be so busy packing that I will probably not see you again until the little boat starts for Tiptonville. Good-bye."

"Auntie is most disturbed," commented Miss Antoinette.

"What's the trouble?" asked the Englishman.

"You wouldn't understand if I told you. Do you know I think Englishmen are the most stupid persons in the world? Why, Mallory and John saw what was the trouble with us girls right away and they have just been wonderful."

"My word! You make me feel—" But he never finished that sentence, for Miss Antoinette jumped up and faced him.

She cried, "If you dare to say 'wilted lettuce' again, I'm going to scream or do something worse. I think without exception you are the dumbest coldest most stupid man that ever was created and you have just about made, poor Aunt Charlotte half insane over you."

She left the room.

"Ormond," asked Sir Harry, "do you know what these women are talking about?"

"I don't know and I don't care," growled Ormond. "I think you have acted like a fool in giving in to these dwarfs the way you have. We might have made a fight for it. Think how it makes me look. Going back to Washington and New York and telling them that we left you here for the rest of your life, practically a prisoner.

"They will ask where our guns were and why didn't we make a fight and I will have to say, 'Oh! Yes, we had fire-arms. Why, I had an elephant gun and Sir Harry wouldn't let me use it!' Think of it! Carrying that gun from New York here and back to New York again and never having a chance to make use of it! All you have told me to do the last month was just to take care of the ladies and make them happy and take them on picnics. And—oh hell!"

BRUNTON spent the rest of the day and much of that night in conference with Mallory Wright over his report. There were things that he wanted told and other things that he felt had better be ignored. The big thing was the fact that the human race was safe, at least for the time being.

The next day came, as all do, at the end of twenty-four hours. The six companions walked down the earthen steps to the boat. Their baggage had been carried there earlier in the day. Orders had been given that during those minutes when the five said goodbye to Sir Harry they were to be left alone.

It was a great day, and the two girls and the New Yorkers were almost jolly in spite of their sadness over leaving Sir Harry. A double wedding was to be celebrated in New York as early that fall as arrangements could be made for it. The four young people were very much in love. They stepped into the boat, rearranged their baggage, and waited for Miss Charlotte. She stood on the bottom step, alongside Sir Harry.

"Come on, Auntie," cried the girls.

Just then the boat started to leave the shore.

"You'll have to hurry," cried Wright.

But the little lady scientist simply smiled and drew nearer to the Englishman's side. Twenty feet of water lay between the boat and the step.

"Goodbye, girls," Miss Carter said gayly. "Give my love to the family and I hope the four of you will be very happy."

"But what are you going to do?" shouted one of the girls.

The little lady made a speaking trumpet out of her hands as she shouted back over the water, *"What-does-it-look-like?"*

"My word! Miss Charlotte, what does it mean?"

She looked up at his bewildered face and smiled as she stroked his arm. "It means that I am going to stay with you—all your life—here or on any other planet—and I am doing it because I love you—you poor stupid dear."

"Do you know how this makes me feel?"

"Oh! I suppose like wilted lettuce or overripe strawberries or something but I hope that you soon will feel like—a man in love. You do love me, don't you, Harry?"

"My word. Yes. *Yes!* Let's go back to the apartment and start the television things. I want to keep in touch with those young people until they are safe."

Back in the apartment they turned on the picture. The boat was shown, rapidly darting through the water and finally landing at the dock at Tiptonville. The four young folks jumped out, divided the baggage and started to walk down the road. Turning on the sound portion of the machine, Sir Harry and Miss Charlotte heard enough to know that, in spite of regrets over leaving two of the party in the crater, still the four on their way to New York were in the best of spirits.

Suddenly there came from the screen the sound of a loud baying and from over the crest of a hill a savage dog ran rapidly toward the little group of travelers. John Ormond fell on one knee, swung around his elephant gun, took aim and fired. The dog disappeared with the explosion. Ormond stood up and started to smile as he patted the gun lovingly.

"*Oh!* This adventure is ending *perfectly!*" cried Miss Charlotte as she threw her arms around her man. "Just think! All six of us going to marry and poor John Ormond finally had a chance to use that gun."

"Righto!" agreed the Englishman, kissing her.

"And perhaps when we all gather for a grand reunion," said the little lady scientist from Virginia as she buried her face in her lover's coat, "perhaps we can get him to tell our grandchildren how he killed an elephant, Harry, dear."

"My word!" said the Englishman as he scattered kisses on her white hair. "You make me feel like a Conqueror."

And he turned off the television.

THE END

www.ingramcontent.com/pod-product-compliance
Lightning Source LLC
Chambersburg PA
CBHW030311180626
46810CB00003B/1018